# *Midley*
# The Settlers

## Emma Batten

All rights reserved

No part of this publication may be reproduced, stored in a retrieval system, or transmitted in any form or by any means without the prior permission in writing of the publisher, nor be otherwise circulated in any form of binding or cover other than that in which it is published and without a similar condition including this condition being impose d on the subsequent purchaser.

The moral right of the author has been asserted.

First published in the UK by Emma Batten.

ISBN 978-1-7399854-4-8

Edited by Debbie Rigden

Further editing and proofreading by Michael Golding, Liz Hopkin & Maud Matley

Cover painting by Kean Farrelly

Printed by Printed World Publishing, Hastings

www.emmabattenauthor.com

For Debbie,

With thanks for all the inconsistencies you spot, your amazing ability to recall what I have, or have not, written in earlier chapters, and for sharing your local knowledge with me.

You have supported me and my writing from the very beginning, first as a reader and then editor, and I love working with you as each new story comes to life.

# Introduction

Welcome to Middle Isle, or Midley as we call it today.

Come with me all the way back to the 11th century when the River Rother cut through Walland Marsh and met the sea at the new port of Romney. Lydd and Romney were separated by the wide estuary, and between them there was a small uninhabited island.

Was it uninhabited? It is mentioned in the Domesday Survey, but historians have doubted that this is our Midley on Romney Marsh. For the sake of my plot, I have chosen for the island to be unoccupied at the beginning of the story.

Lydd is usually shown as an island on maps of this period, but I have seen images of a shingle ridge from Pett Level to Dungeness. Again, for the sake of the plot, I have chosen to allow access to Lydd by land.

The characters in this novel are all fictional, while the places are as realistic as possible.

# Meg at Rype

## Lydd
## Late Winter 1085

Four strangers arrived in our town today. They came in peace, yet caused unrest amongst us, and I am certain their coming will play a part in the long story of Lydd.

Nineteen years have passed since William of Normandy became our King. In that time his men have never troubled us, our town being nothing but a humble place set between a shingle promontory and bleak marshland. Now the King's men have purposely sought us out and there must be some reason for them being here. Lydd is not a place you merely come across. They were bound for our town and found it.

These Normans have taken such an interest in us, such care to record every detail, that it seems our town will now be known throughout the Kingdom.

Whereas before, King William and his men only knew of nearby Romney, now they will learn about Lydd.

I should be afraid of what their attention will bring, yet I feel an excitement... an anticipation simmering within me. But I am moving too fast and must tell you what happened from the beginning.

*

They came from the direction of Broomhill and were first seen by Richard Woodman and his son, Richard the Younger, our nearest neighbours who live in a tiny, thatched cottage on the outer reaches of our settlement. My father and I were tending our land – he digging manure into the stony, brown soil, and I pulling at scrappy leeks and stunted turnips – when Richard the Younger came tumbling into view.

"He trips when there is nothing to trip over!" Father let out a burst of laughter, having paused in his labours and straightened his back to observe the boy stumbling towards us.

"Martin at Rype... Martin..." Richard the Younger shouted. "Thank God I was up thatching the roof... Thank the Lord I happened to look that way. The Normans are coming! By horseback. They come by horseback and will be upon us in no time."

"How many?" Father barked back at him. "How far away?"

"Four! One on a white horse."

I remember wondering why the colour of the beast mattered.

"Not yet at Broomhill, but not far from it," Richard continued.

"Four," Father repeated. "Not an army, but Normans, nonetheless. There may be others behind them. We must spread the word and spread it fast. Make haste, Richard, and I will join you after I have settled things here." Then he turned to me and continued, "Meg, these men will think nothing of setting fire to our home and killing our animals. Douse the fire, so they have no ready flames to hand, and free the goats. Then fill a sack with whatever you hold most precious and run for the church. And when you are there… pray… pray they show us mercy for there is nothing here of any value to them."

By now Richard the Younger had fled, taking the track into town.

"What will you do?" I asked, following my father as he strode into a storeroom attached to the mud and straw walls of our cottage. He didn't reply but took his strongest knife and added it to his belt, then reached for the scythe used for cutting reeds. There was no need for him to respond as his intention became clear. My father was preparing to fight those four Normans and any others in their wake.

His next words may have seemed irrelevant, but I understood the meaning: "Tie back your hair, Meg. Cover it. It is too pretty." He expected blood to be shed at the hands of these strangers and for any comely woman to be at their mercy. Then he was gone, his final words being, "Hurry. Do as I say, then hasten to the church."

As he spoke, the church bell began to toll. At that moment, we knew Richard the Younger had reached the town and alerted Amory of Langport. The bell called for the people of the parish to gather.

*Fire. Hair. Goats.* The words ran over and over in my mind as I snatched at the bucket of freshly drawn water and doused the fire before scattering the damp logs across the pit. Then I opened the trunk by my bed and took a length of ribbon. Without pulling a comb through my thick golden curls, I tied them at the nape of my neck. Next, I took a light shawl and placed it over my head. My good, thick shawl I wrapped around my shoulders.

*What else should I take? What might we need?* In a canvas bag, I placed my comb and my mother's brooch, which in turn nestled in an embroidered purse. *What else?* Thick stockings hung from a rack by the fire alongside a hemp shift; folding them quickly, I pushed them into the bag. *Does Father mean me to pack something for him? Food, or a pan?*

4

I couldn't think what was needed. How could I when I didn't know what terrible fate I was meant to be preparing for? So, I left home, thinking that once outside, my mind would clear, and it would only take a moment to dash back and fill the bag.

Racing across scrappy grass, past our woodpile and the manure heap, I shooed at the chickens. Although they were scrawny, one bird would offer a hearty meal for hungry Normans. Then I was tugging at the twine securing the gate to a fence post while the largest and boldest nanny goat pressed her head against the gate, hindering my efforts.

The goats kicked at the thin grass underfoot, threw their heads back and were gone before I could even think of slapping their rumps. All they thought of was the lush grass and tender shoots of greenery elsewhere and now they had their chance to explore beyond the confines of our pasture. They would return, as they always did. They were determined beasts and often escaped.

*How much longer?* I looked to the south-west and felt my body chill then stiffen. Figures on horseback were approaching. Without stopping to count them, or to be sure of them being Normans, I grabbed at the bag and ran towards the town. It wasn't far and, keeping a steady pace, I covered open land before reaching the next cottage, and then the next. Now the buildings came one after the other and I joined the women and children all heading for the church.

On a triangle of land, between two tracks which meet close to our church, the men gathered, brandishing flails, axes and lengths of wood. In their midst, Father appeared to be poised for battle. Our leader, Amory of Langport, stood barking commands. Before I reached the churchyard, they had set off along the track which eventually led to Broomhill and then the Camber bank, that long finger of land between the sea and treacherous marshland.

*They will meet with the Normans in no time at all, possibly before they reach the town boundaries.*

The very sight of our ancient church gave me comfort. Its stone walls are three times higher than any other building in our town and have already stood for hundreds of years. Those people who settled after the Romans must have thought Lydd to be special when they brought stone here to create a sacred place. The Normans think differently as they favour the new port at Romney with a holy edifice and have taken no notice of us. At least not until now.

I stray. This is my account of today and the coming of the Normans – there is no time to waste on olden days people or a place I will never see and the stories of its church.

Father and I live on the outer reaches of the town, and it seemed as if I was the last woman to reach the church as I raced past mounds of buried kinsmen and almost threw myself at the oak door, lifting the latch and pushing on the weathered planks. It did not shift. I tried again. No movement.

"Who is it?" a woman called, her voice shaky. I believed it to be Philippa, wife of Amory.

"Meg!" I called. "Meg. Martin at Rype's daughter. I had further to come."

Metal slid against metal as the bolt was released. I pressed through the slit of a space they allowed me before slamming the door behind me. Darkness closed in on me, while the odour of damp stone and wood hung thick in the air. I breathed deeply, finding it comforting.

"Did you see them?"

"Are the men ready?"

I moved through the nave, using the small, high windows as a guide, then passed through an archway into an aisle before responding, "I saw them – the Normans. Our men were gathered and moved away before I reached churchyard."

Opinions flew about. Some whispered, others spoken with the confidence of people who know nothing. None of these women knew what our fate was. We could only pray that the four Normans and the army we assumed followed in their wake would be lenient on us.

Squatting on the ground, with my arms wrapped around my canvas bag, I closed my eyes. "Lord in heaven, may you look down upon us with kindness and mercy..."

# Martin at Rype

I am ashamed. Humiliated.

When word came to us about the approaching Normans, I could only think that they wished us harm. In my mind I saw them rampaging through Lydd, destroying our homes, slaying our animals, satisfying their lust with our women. No sooner than Richard the Younger had blurted the news, and I allowed terror to rise unchecked within me.

I acted without reason.

There were four Normans. Four. Yet, due to my actions, when they reached the town boundary, they met with over forty men of Lydd. Each one of those forty brandished a weapon of sorts. Each one had allowed fear to rule him.

Those Normans did no more than command their horses to stop and raise their hands in a gesture to show they came in peace.

Amory stepped forward and called to us, "Put your weapons down. These men are no threat to us." With this he laid his stout pole on the ground and raised his hand. "Greetings. What brings you here? It is not the time of year to be travelling."

Their spokesman dismounted and he too moved forward. "Greetings to you and the brave men of this town. We come from the court of King William and have been travelling for a whole cycle of the moon. The King wishes for there to be a record of every town and village in England. We are here to learn about your settlement."

"Every town and village!" Amory repeated. "How can it be done?"

"It shall be done," the Norman stated. "All we ask of you is that we are provided with a table to lay our sheets of vellum upon, and shelter for the night. We see this is a humble place and will happily bed down in a barn or in your church."

"And food," one of the strangers called out, his tone friendly. "Food for us and our horses."

"Of course," Amory replied. "Food is sparse at this time of year, but we can feed both you and your beasts." He turned to face the men of Lydd, running his gaze from one face to the next. "Martin at Rype," he said, raising his voice a little.

"Aye." My right arm was behind my back, my fingers curled around the handle of the scythe. It was an awkward weapon to hide, unlike the knife nestling beneath the folds of my tunic.

"Clear the church. Ask my wife to provide a meal for our visitors."

"I'll do that."

Later, when our guests are settled and the townsfolk have returned to their daily tasks, will our leader, Amory, remember who ignited this flame of fear amongst us? I am certain he will.

# *Meg*

One moment I was praying that the Normans would spare our lives and homes, the next my father was at the church door.

"Draw back the bolts!" he called. "We have nothing to fear. They want no more than food, shelter and to learn about our town."

"But the army..." Philippa's voice quivered as she slid the bolt back.

"Four men. Just four," my father replied. I thought he should have sounded joyous, but instead there was a flatness to his voice.

Unable to see him, I edged forward, slipping between the elders of our town then narrowing my eyes as I looked towards the doorway. In the sunlight, I could not make out his features but saw the slump to his shoulders.

"They ask for no more than a table to write at, food for themselves and their horses, and somewhere to shelter for the night. Amory asked that you, Philippa, provide a meal. They can sleep and work here in the church."

"What do they want with us?" someone called out. "Why do they come here to write?"

"To make a record of what they find out," Father replied. "We will learn more soon enough. You women and children can leave the church and go back to your homes or work." With that he turned away, no doubt wanting to return to the men and catch up on whatever news the Normans had to share.

Without waiting to see if Philippa needed me, I left the church, immediately moving away from the gathering of men and heading towards the river. I met no one as I hurried along a narrow track, taking care not to slip on the ribbons of exposed shingle or hard, bare earth. In no time at all the Rother was stretching out before me, the tide low, and exposed mud banks glittering with shards of ice. Hardy waterside plants, which tolerated being drenched by saltwater and the seemingly relentless winds, drooped in a near lifeless state while awaiting the spring.

I paused to catch my breath then, turning to the south-west, took the path used by fishermen. Upon reaching the area where they kept a couple of small boats along with their tackle, I turned inland. My roundabout route took me past no more than a couple of shacks and I was soon back safely on

Father's land at the edge of an expanse of rough pasture called the Rype.

This common land is the playground for our goats who, when released from their pen, return with udders swollen, providing milk for us. Later in their lives, God willing that they live to a good age, there is meat for our cooking pot. The soil on the Rype lies thin and sandy. It is mean ground with none of the richness found in our land nearer the Rother. There, the waterway, over thousands of years, has left valuable sediments. Father experiments with his planting of crops as he attempts to grow the lushest greens and plumpest root vegetables alongside oats and barley. Yet most of our land is different again being meagre soil, overrun with stones and fed with manure from our chickens and goats. We manage to farm the best we can and are grateful to be able to exchange our produce for fish which improves our diet and is plentiful throughout the seasons.

Now you have a picture of our land at that time when the four Normans came, so I will continue with my tale of returning home.

Hastening back home had warmed me, and my mind had been filled with our visitors and their reasons for being here, but now I had to deal with the consequences of Father's rash reaction to them coming. To see the fire a sodden, grey mass in its pit was disheartening. Dropping the canvas bag on my bed, I left the cottage for the store where I picked up a bucket. Then I retreated to the firepit, knelt on the earth floor and scraped out the wet ashes, setting aside any part-burned wood that could be salvaged.

Thanks to the many weeks of dry, albeit icy, weather my collection of dry reed heads, leaves and twigs was soon tempted to burst into flame, and I continued to nurse the fire in between adding turnips and leeks to yesterday's broth, now turned solid. When Father returned home, a hearty meal would improve his temper.

With the gravy in the pot bubbling away, I turned my attention to the bag, still lying on my low bed of rough blankets on a flattened straw mattress.

"What use would this have been?" I murmured to myself, tipping the contents onto my bed. Comb. Brooch. Stockings. Shift. "What use would this be if we had lost everything else?" I tore the ribbon from my hair, letting it tumble across my shoulders. The scrap of fabric, I threw on the bed with the meagre collection of my belongings.

"Did you douse the fire earlier?" my father asked, eyeing the smouldering logs and bubbling pot with suspicion.

"I did everything you asked," I replied, my attention on the flatbread as I flipped it in the pan.

"There was no army," he stated, hanging his thick cape on a peg. "They didn't come to harm us."

"Why did they come?" I asked. Father was clearly in a black mood, and I hoped the interest stirred by strangers coming to our town might lift that darkness.

"It's quite a thing they are doing," he began, accepting a beaker of ale. "The King wants to know what we have. What every village and town has. Land, tools, animals…"

"Everything?" I queried as we settled at the table with our meal.

"Ploughs. Big tools." He left out a guffaw. "I told them we don't have much use for a plough here – too stony!"

"They spoke to everyone?"

"Nay, the freemen of the town. Those with a bit of land. All twenty-one of us had to line up and then go and tell them. But they want to know about everyone." He dunked his bread into the broth, letting it soak up the liquid, and lifted it, dripping, to his mouth.

I allowed him the pleasure of eating. It had been some time since our last meal, and I was glad of the distraction. While we dipped and spooned and slurped, I considered this information. All I could think over and over was how could this be possible? How could the King's men seek out every pig… every ox... every horse? How could King William ever hope to learn how each area of meadow, marshland and woodland was used? These men sent to find out... how could they be certain of finding every place in the country? By the time my bowl was wiped clean, I had almost given up. I have seen so little of the world beyond our town and cannot hope to understand how such a project could be attempted. So, I merely asked, "They want to know what everyone has, when some people have nothing of worth?"

"If those people have nothing, then the Normans still want to know it," Father confirmed. "It's the money, you see."

"There's not much of that," I replied. Food, tools and animals usually changed hands without coins as we bartered amongst ourselves.

"It still has a value," Father stood, indicating that he was almost done with this talk of the Normans and their survey, "and our King wants to know that he is having his share."

"And if the church is having theirs?" I queried. Canterbury, a place I could only imagine, owned all the land hereabouts.

"He wants to know all about us," Father confirmed. Moving to the doorway, he took his cloak from the peg. "The day has been wasted – the goats still need milking, and the chickens are running loose. Darkness will soon be upon us. Why did they choose to come when the days are so short – do they think we have nothing else to do but answer their questions? I'll start the milking... if the beasts have had the sense to come home."

His last words trailed away as Father left and the heavy curtain covering the doorway fell back into place. He was right to think the goats would return, but I knew that the task of securing the chickens overnight would be frustrating and largely pointless. Having made the fire safe and wiped our wooden bowls clean, I pulled my cloak from its peg and trudged outside, my thoughts absorbed with the vastness of King William's lands and wondering why he would have any interest in our desolate spot.

# Meg

News of a meeting reached me in the marketplace today as I exchanged a jar of honey for a pair of flounder. The trade was a fair one, and it pleased me to feel the weight of the fish in my basket.

"Your father will be there," Daniel by Rother stated now the deal was complete. "He'll be one of the first to know what all this is about." He jerked his head in the direction of our stone church. "Him and the other freemen of the town."

"If there's a meeting, Father will be there." I shrugged. "You'll give me the jar back, won't you?"

We both glanced at the earthenware pot still clasped in his hand.

"Of course. I'll leave it by your door."

Irritated by this brief exchange of words, I turned away, but Daniel was not done with me. "Meg," he called. "Meg!"

Swivelling to face him, I said nothing, but my hesitation gave Daniel the confidence to continue, "I hope there's good news for us here in Lydd. It's been a long winter, and I'm fearful of trouble ahead."

"I won't be there," I reminded him, unnecessarily. With that I picked up my pace. A scowl settled on my face, tightening my jaw and pulling my lips into a pout. What right did Daniel have to speak of a meeting between the freemen? It was not for him to speculate on the town's business, but to fish the tidal waters of the Rother as his father had and his father before him. My bad temper was unreasonable, and I knew it was not Daniel who caused it with his gossip, but my disgraced father who had withheld the news.

That is how I heard news of the gathering of freemen to be held in the church tomorrow.

"I hear there is to be a meeting," I said while preparing the fish for the pan. Keeping my eyes firmly upon the flesh, taking care not to break the bones, I waited. My father had been irritable over the past few days, tending to stay close to home and not wanting to leave our land or speak to anyone who passed by.

"Aye, there's to be a meeting."

I skinned the fillet and waited.

"Amory of Langport sent a message," Father continued. "The freemen are to meet at church in the morning. I can't think what he wants." With that he muttered something about fetching more wood for the fire and left. It was clear that I would learn no more until tomorrow.

# *Martin*

I can't speak about what happened at the meeting. I *won't* speak of it yet.

What I will say is that I know why Amory chose me – he wants rid of me. It is because of the Normans, of course, and now Amory has come up with a scheme to have me gone from Lydd. He does not wish to be reminded of how I called the men to arms and made them look like fools.

I am humiliated. Disgraced.

His plan is good, and I can see the merit in it. If it were my idea, then I would be proud of it and glad to leave on this adventure. But it was not my idea.

Soon I will tell Meg. How will she feel when she knows of my leaving and her staying behind? Amory has thought of this and offered his widowed sister as a companion for my daughter who I am sure will be grateful. Life would be lonely for Meg without some company, and I would worry to think of her being alone.

When I am gone, I will endeavour to earn Amory of Langport's respect and hope to return triumphant.

# Meg

I can hardly believe the amount of news and gossip that flies about the town now. The two become mingled until no one knows the truth. The latest came from Father when he returned from the meeting with the other freemen.

"I am being sent to Middle Isle!" he announced the moment he was near enough to share the news.

"Middle Isle?" I echoed. A ripple of excitement flew through my body. "For what reason?"

No one ever speaks of going to that mystical, shifting island in the wide waters of the Rother. Although people must have been there, for it is no distance at all by boat. They must have been, yet never talk of it. I mention it being nearby and at times it seems that I can see the shape of each tree in the small copse and the gentle rise of the land, sloping up to the north-east. But more often the Isle shimmers grey and purple, its features indistinct on the bright, warm days. Then on the dull days it lurks amongst the mists, swaying with them and edging further away. Sometimes, although I know it is there,

22

the Isle seems to have gone altogether and, however much I strain my eyes, nothing can be seen.

"Why?" I asked, standing with a stone in my hand and a small barrow to my side. I had been watching for Father while clearing our fields with the poor soil; working and watching as the sun passed its highest point and was halfway towards settling for the night. Observing his progress, I had seen from his long stride and rounded shoulders that his temper had not improved. But I had to know, and so I repeated, "Why send you to Middle Isle? Not because... not because of the Normans? It was Richard the Younger who was the first to spread the news. Is he going?"

"If you stop all your chatter, then you'll learn sooner."

I waited.

"It's this survey," Father began, reaching down to pick up a smooth pebble. "Amory was ashamed of what they learnt about us. That's how it all began."

"Ashamed?"

"We have six ploughlands – just six for growing crops. So much of our soil is too stony." He tossed the pebble into the barrow. "We know that as well as anyone. There is no woodland, other than the holly on the shingle, and we cannot claim to own any elsewhere. Amory is embarrassed by the little we have."

"We have a stone church," I reminded him.

"Our King cannot take taxes from a church." Father considered this for a moment. "Besides, the Romans built it. We can take no credit."

Leaning down, I took the handles of the barrow and began to trundle it across the field. The stones danced as the crude wheel rolled over ruts, and Father added more to the pile as we headed home.

Picking stones from the thin, dark soil is both thankless and compulsive. A never-ending quantity work their way to the surface, so our task is never completed, but I feel myself compelled to keep removing the largest and the lumpiest of them. Often my barrow fills beyond what is sensible and, as I push the heavy load, they bounce about, some scattering back onto the land.

"We have salt houses," I said, having carefully considered what our town could take some pride in.

"We do, and seven of them! Lydd does well for salt and fisheries."

But we had strayed. All this talk of what a poor place our town is distracted me from the news of Father going to Midley. How odd my thoughts are, flitting from one thing to another.

"You are actually going to Middle Isle?" I questioned, needing to know but nervous of his response.

"Amory has decreed that the soil there is fertile, and we would be wise to make use of it. He wants to send a small group of us there to prepare the land, plant seeds and tend the crops."

Now we were close to home, and Father took the barrow from me, pushing it over the hardened earth in our area between the cottage, outbuildings and animal pens. He tipped the stones onto the pile collected over the past months and they tumbled about. The barrow was propped against the woodstore, and he continued: "It has been decided that we can gain two, perhaps three, ploughlands on the island if the land is worked from now until Michaelmas. From planting to harvest, Amory wants the land watched and managed."

"You are going there to stay!" I began to understand the enormity of his news. Now a hundred thoughts rattled about in my head, and I blurted the most pressing of them all, "Am I going too? Will I go to Middle Isle?"

"Of course not," Father's response was immediate. "You are needed here to care for our land and beasts."

"On my own?"

"You will have help. Amory has thought of that. He has no reason to punish you."

"Punish? What is this talk of punishing?" My words flew out far more forcibly than intended.

Father ignored my reaction as he moved towards the first of the places where the free-roaming chickens were known to lay. "Joan will come to stay. I think Amory is pleased to be rid of her, and she will be useful to you. She is a sensible woman."

He spoke of our leader's sister who had been widowed last summer. Suddenly, and without warning, the yearning for another woman's company – a motherly figure – swept over me. My own mother, a hazy memory, had passed from this earth when I was a child of ten years. I had lived half my lifetime without her. Other than the rhythm of the changing seasons, little altered from week to week, month to month. Now I pictured welcoming Joan to my home and introducing her to the work needing to be done on the land, but mostly I thought of her companionship. The evenings would be filled with the possibilities of learning more about life beyond Lydd as there had been a period during her marriage when Joan had settled elsewhere.

Trailing after Father, my mind busy with new thoughts, I was brought back to the present when he tutted for the third or fourth time, still having not found an egg. They were sparse in the winter, but we hoped to find some to barter with. "I can't manage on my own and it seems like a good choice," I said. "Shall I go and see her? Does she know? When will it be?"

"Ah!" Father exclaimed as he spotted an egg. "Go to see Joan tomorrow or the next day. She will have been told. Three weeks, Amory told us. There is much to prepare, and by then the coldest of the weather will have passed."

"I'll do that."

Later, as supper simmered over the fire, I skipped out of our home and walked briskly towards the river, eager to get a glance of the Isle before nightfall. The late afternoon was oddly windless, but the freezing air nipped at my nose and cheeks while the rest of my slender figure remained snug, swathed in layers of wool. At the water's edge, I saw Daniel by Rother hauling his small craft onto the mud bank. Neither of us acknowledged the other, and I moved further to the east, wanting to absorb the enchantment of the place without interruption. Within moments, I stood alone, my shoes sinking slightly into the soft, gravelly beach, and my attention settled on Middle Isle.

The island squatted low with the grey tidal waters sliding sluggishly past. It told me nothing about what it might offer to my father and the others who would make it their home for the coming seasons. I lingered and willed it to divulge something – I would like to have seen a strong outline of some trees, a flock of birds rising, the shape of the island revealed... A mist rolled in from the west. The already weak sun became shrouded, and I stood stock-still, compelled to watch Middle Isle fade away.

With my body now stiff from the cold and realising that the mist was thickening at an alarming rate, I turned and made a hasty retreat towards the warmth of home.

# Meg

It is all arranged. Father is to leave the day after tomorrow and will not return until after the crops have been harvested on Middle Isle. Over the last ten days his ill temper has passed, and he now sees himself as essential to the success of the project. His knowledge of soils and crops is much admired here, and Amory has tasked him with providing the seeds and tools. Not only will we use our own carefully selected supplies, but Father can ask any landowner to donate to the project and, by order of Amory of Langport, they must!

Without seeing Middle Isle for himself, Father has considered the soil and is certain he will find it rich with deposits from the sea.

"It will be salty though, Meg," he has said over and over. "Salty in the air and the soil. We must choose plants which are tolerant of those conditions."

It was 'we' – Father and I – whose days were filled with discussing the volume, quality and type of seeds to take. Peas were placed in a hessian bag, but not beans which were known to grow weakly in the salt air. In small, wooden boxes we placed turnip, carrot, parsnip and leek seeds. The onions, already formed as bulbs, nestled in their own sack.

"Picks, axes, spades, rakes..."

Father lists tools as we settle by the fire in the evening. "Each one must be checked thoroughly and repaired by the smithy if needed. It would be a shame to be hindered by an inferior piece of equipment just as we are starting out."

When he is not speaking of the seeds, the tools and the order of planting, Father discusses the others who have been selected to leave our shore for Middle Isle. He sees himself as the leader, and only when the monk is mentioned, does he doubt his position.

"He is expected to work with the rest of us," Father reminds me, although I hear the uncertainty in his tone. "Friar Matthew will have his duties to the Lord and must show his devotion as well as tending to our spiritual needs. But this will not take all his time and he has been told... I am sure he has been told... that every man and woman who settles on Middle Isle will be there to work for the good of us all."

"The action of tilling the soil can be soothing and the repetitive nature of the work lends itself to holy contemplation." I attempt to reassure Father.

"The friar can do both," he agrees.

We feel fortunate that the wandering monk, Friar Matthew, arrived in Lydd last autumn. Without him, the settlers would have been forced to live without any religious influence. There is only one priest in Lydd and the people of Denge have none so must travel to our church.

I wonder if the monk feels so fortunate – perhaps he has plans to continue his journey to places where he may attract a greater flock? Or does he feel favoured to have this opportunity to bless the virgin land when the first of the seeds are sown? I find myself pondering on this a lot and look forward to sharing my thoughts with another woman when Joan of Langport comes to stay with me.

Daniel by Rother will also be a part of the group. His boat will take the settlers to the Isle. Perhaps his father and uncle will also be involved in transporting tools, the material for shelters, the food and cooking utensils across the water, as the family own two small vessels. Daniel will be loaded with poles and nets for he intends to set up keddle net fishing, as well as using his spearing expertise to catch eels. When we speak of the practical details of living on Middle Isle, there is no doubt that the sea will provide the mainstay of their diet.

The new land will provide no sustenance until the crops are sown and harvested. Philippa of

Langport is to organise a weekly collection of grain, ale and vegetables, but there may be times when the weather and tides make the crossing dangerous for Daniel and they may have to wait for their food.

Who else will be setting off to Middle Isle? Each man and woman has been carefully chosen by Amory. The land will, at first, have so little to give, so every settler must bring with them skills and experience. The first of the married couples are John Smithy and his wife Eve. "We have much to do and cannot afford to be hindered by a loose nail or broken iron band," Father says when he speaks of the decision to take the smithy with them. "It will be quite a task for he must take the tools of his trade and plenty of charcoal – that will be one trip for Daniel, just to take the pair of them over!"

John and Eve are free to leave their sons, one of them also named John, to tend the permanent forge in our town, and John the Younger's wife can run the home. It is an arrangement everyone is happy with, Eve told me when we exchanged our news in the marketplace. "We've never been across the water, not to Romney nor Rye," she said. "Denge and Broomhill – John goes there plenty with his work, but there's never been a reason to go further."

The second married couple, Edwin and Sarah Carpenter, raise much debate within our home or when Father and I work on the land together. "Too young," he stated within a day of learning who his companions would be. "I don't understand our leader's thinking there."

"But Daniel by Rother is young," I reminded him. "He is two years older than me, I believe."

"Daniel goes unencumbered."

"Unencumbered by a wife?"

"That's right. What if Sarah is with child?" he asked, his tone sharp.

I pondered on this for a moment and have continued to think about it over the past three weeks. But I have faith in Amory who always shows that he has the good of our town in his mind.

"Then that is how it will be, and they will manage," I suggested. "Eve will be there with her experience of raising four healthy children, and her knowledge of remedies. She will care for them all and, if needed, she will help Sarah if she carries a child."

"But Sarah is needed to work the land and cook for us."

"Then she will do both, as women have done throughout time." Father tended to fuss over the smallest of details, while I was used to reacting calmly and often changing the subject. "Edwin is a fine carpenter," I reminded him. "He has been taught by his father and uncle, and they are both worthy choices for the Middle Isle tasks. However, a younger man is needed to haul wood about, and even then Edwin will need Daniel's or John's help at times. He is a good choice."

Now we are so occupied by Middle Isle that I wonder what we ever found to talk about before this great adventure was planned. Wherever I go, the townspeople want to speak to me about our preparations and they ask how Father feels – is he uneasy or eager to be going there? I am left to make inadequate responses. It may seem strange – it does seem strange, even to me – but I feel that this is just as much my journey, and every day I look forward to the changes coming to my life. Despite the damp days, I have washed and aired blankets for Joan's bed and tidied our home the best I can. It is not easy – the seeds and tools are piling up, threatening to spill across the whole room. Everything is ready and now we must wait. Only the weather can stop Daniel by Rother, his father and uncle ferrying the settlers across to the Isle.

# Martin

"Christ's nails!" I've never known such pain – it sears through my body as if the flames of hell consume me. My mind cannot focus on what must be done or indeed how to do it. And now I sweat...

The roof needed repairing. But what a fool I was to think of setting up the ladder and climbing onto it without my daughter or a local man to help. Meg could have dealt with it – I could have asked her to speak with Ned Thatcher and arrange for him to come. He would have been glad to help.

Now my mind wanders... and I feel the icy fingers of the coastal winds wrap themselves around me.

I would welcome sleep.

# Daniel by Rother

Meg came to see me early this morning. I'd never known her to seek me out and hoped that whatever she wanted I could be of some use… some help to her. Watching her striding over the tussocks and skirting the ribbons of shingle, I felt nervous of the news she brought.

"Daniel!" she called. "I need to speak to you."

I walked towards her, my boots squelching in the mud of the tidal creek, then picked up my pace the best I could. As she neared me, I could see the exhaustion in Meg's face and that her usual rosy bloom was no longer apparent. Yet, despite there appearing to be something very wrong, there was a peculiar gleam in her eyes, and this struck me as being odd.

"It's Father," she began. "Everything has changed, and I came to tell you first because you are a part of it... Amory must be told next, but he – Father, I mean – asked me to come to you first..."

Meg had uttered more words that I had ever known her to before, yet told me nothing at all. I waited.

"He's broken his leg," she explained. "It's bad, Daniel, and will take some months to heal. Even then, it may not be as it was before."

Reflecting on her first words 'everything has changed', I couldn't help but wonder how this would alter our plans. Martin is, or was, the leader amongst the settlers bound for Middle Isle; not that we ever named him that, but it is understood. Amory had the idea of growing crops, and Martin was the one to provide the seeds and tools. But it is more than that – he has a wisdom we are relying on.

"How did it happen?" I asked, while numerous possibilities rattled around in my mind.

"The thatch was loose," she told me, her exasperation clear. "Why didn't he wait? What a thing to do, going up there on his own. Someone should have been there to hold the ladder. I would have been back in no time." Meg scowled. "I found him sheltering in the tool shed, with nothing but a piece of sacking to cover him."

"He did it because he couldn't think of leaving unless the home was secure."

Martin at Rype is a man who prefers to cope on his own. I have known him all my life, but rarely exchange more than a word or two with him. That changed recently when there were things to be said... things to be arranged for our new life. He does not invite idle talk, and his daughter is the same. That's how I knew when I saw Meg this morning there was a reason, and an important one, for her coming to see me.

"I know," Meg admitted after considering my response. "But there was no need. I would have dealt with the roof."

There was no doubting she is Martin's daughter, as fiercely independent as he is.

"Is he in much pain?" I asked, wanting to know what this meant for our plans.

"Eve has been and set the leg as best as she can, and David Woodman has brought a temporary crutch until he can make another one to suit Father's height. But the pain... aye, he is in pain, although Eve gave him some remedy to ease it."

We remained standing on the strip of ground between land and waterway, the place where the tide lapped when it reached its highest point. I wondered if I should be inviting Meg back to our home where my mother would make sage tea and ask the right questions. As I dithered, she continued:

"He is not fit to travel. You will have realised that."

38

"Aye."

"So, he says I must go in his place! I am to go to Middle Isle."

Now I understood why, amongst the anxiety, there was a sense of nervous excitement. I found myself questioning Meg, although she had made it clear enough. "Go to Middle Isle? You are to go in his place?" I stopped myself and continued with, "It makes sense. You must know his plans – you have prepared for this together."

"We have," she agreed, her voice high. "We have done nothing else since we knew about settling on the island. Aye, it does make sense. I don't have his strength, but I know my father's plans as well as he does." She paused, as if considering her next words. I waited. "Daniel... would you... would you come with me to speak to Amory? He needs to understand that I must go, and I don't know if he... if he will listen to me."

I'll admit to being surprised by Meg asking this. We have never been friends. Up to this very day, she has seemed aloof, never saying more than needed to be said. Now it seemed that she not only needed to share the news of Martin's accident but wanted my support.

"I'm not a freeman," I reminded her. "My family don't go telling our lord how to do things. We fish."

"Not freemen," she conceded, "but you own boats and do your own trading. That should earn his respect."

Meg is a thinker, and I like that. She was right too. Neither my father nor my uncle are called to the church when the freemen meet, but people speak well of them. More importantly, we are part of the Middle Isle plans. It's an odd thing that no one ever goes to the Isle. No one from Lydd ever thought much of it before. My uncle has circled it in the boat once or twice, and Amory was interested in what he had to say about it. Meg was right; there is respect for my family.

Looking down at my footwear, clogged with mud, I began to wipe it on scraggy clumps of grass. "I'll come with you."

"Thank you."

Meg seemed content with little talk as we tramped side-by-side towards the town. Left to my thoughts, I pondered upon the shift of power within our group of seven men and women. A woman could not be our leader. There are stories through history of powerful women – but not here. Not in Lydd. Not on Romney Marsh. Meg will be respected in our group though. Respected for her knowledge of seeds and planting, as well as being Martin at Rype's daughter.

Once on the island, who will become our natural leader, I wondered. Perhaps John Smithy. I had two reasons to think this: the first was his age, him being a father to grown offspring, and the second was that he is well-liked for being both fair and friendly.

Our path followed the banks of the river, and it wasn't until we reached the first cluster of humble cottages that Meg echoed my thoughts: "Will Amory allow us to go with no freeman? Will he choose someone else to go in Father's place?"

"I would be happy with John Smithy as our leader," I told her. "But perhaps... although there is such little time."

"But we must go tomorrow," she responded, her words coming fast and betraying her fear of being left behind. "If we wait, then perhaps I will not be needed. The urgency will have passed."

A new thought came to mind as she spoke and, without properly replying to her last words, I asked, "How will your father manage? He can't work the land. Can he care for himself even? And your home is away from the rest of the townsfolk, as is my own."

"I must find help before I go," she told me. "I thank God that all the tools... the seeds... everything is ready."

It seems that nothing will stop Meg from going to Middle Isle unless Amory were to decide against it. I find my opinions to be mixed: at first admiring her determination and later thinking her to be ruthless in her choice to leave Martin.

I have voiced it now. Ruthless. A harsh word to use about a beautiful young woman. It is too much – let me reconsider. Perhaps careless, or even wilful, would be more correct. Meg would not plan to leave Martin unless he had people to ensure he was looked after, while the land and animals were tended.

But I have wandered in my thoughts and must return to us finding Amory. Fortunately, as we reached the town, our lord was spotted on the threshold of his longhouse which abutted the churchyard. On seeing us, he raised his arm and beckoned.

"He already knows," Meg realised. "He knows about Father."

"Meg! Daniel." Amory of Langport gestured for us to go into his home.

We followed, this being my first time, and no doubt Meg's, in the longhouse. Stepping in, we found ourselves in the area where animal pens met living area.

"Sit down," Amory offered, as my eyes adjusted to the dimly lit space.

There were three benches not far from the fire and I moved towards one, then gazed up into the eaves space and back down to shuttered windows and along to curtains stretching the width of the room. That's where Amory and Philippa have their bed, behind the curtains, and maybe his sister too. The servants must sleep on the floor by the fire or in the loft above the animals.

It is nothing to do with me where they sleep, so back to what happened when he spoke to Meg.

"How's Martin?" he asked.

"His leg is painful," she responded. "And he's worried about our plans. That's why I'm here. We are hoping, Father and I, that I can go to Middle Isle in his place. I know all his plans, you see. It is all we have spoken about in the last three weeks. We have decided exactly when each seed will be sown and I understand there may be different types of soil there, and which is best for each type of planting..." Her words had been rushed and now Meg waited. I could sense she was holding her breath.

Amory looked at me. "What brings you here, Daniel?"

"Meg came to tell me about Martin, and..." I faltered now, not recalling if she had asked my opinion, or merely told me of her plans. "I suggested that I come along with her. She's experienced in the growing of crops, and I know she's a hard worker, so it seems..."

She shot me a smile, knowing my response was not entirely truthful.

"Since I heard the news of Martin's accident, I have been determined that nothing will stop the settlers from leaving for Middle Isle tomorrow," Amory admitted. "Ever since the Normans came, I have resolved to extend our land." He paused, considering his next words, then continued, "My sister can care for Martin and the home, but we need a man to work your land. Joan cannot do everything."

"I would have welcomed her to keep me company," Meg admitted, her tone sombre, "but will gladly go to Middle Isle, if you agree. And a man, or boy, can work our land under Father's instruction, so he needn't be skilled."

"To be young and strong would be best," I added.

It seemed that it was all agreed. Perhaps Amory had even thought of this himself, as it seemed that nothing much had been discussed or fully agreed, and our lord was standing as if our audience with him was finished.

"Well, aye, that's all fine," Amory concluded, walking towards the door. "But now we need another man. Martin would have tilled the land all day long, and you, Meg, do not have the same strength."

"Could I suggest my uncle's second son, Luke, to come to Midley?" I asked. "He can dig, as well as handle a boat and help with fishing if needed."

"I'll leave it to you to ask him," Amory said. Now we were all standing on the road outside the

44

longhouse. "Meg – tell your father that you are to go to the Isle. And tell him... tell him that I hope his leg heals without trouble."

"It may never be as it was before," Meg replied. "The bones may not set straight. That's Eve's opinion and we can only hope she is wrong." She stopped abruptly, then added, "Although I respect her knowledge."

A man's path can change in an instant. Yesterday Martin at Rype began his day as leader of our group of seven. Tomorrow Martin's strength will be replaced by my cousin, Luke, and his skills by his own daughter, Meg. Tomorrow eight of us will set out for Middle Isle.

# Martin

Damn my misfortune. What sort of father am I, sitting here with my leg propped up, as my daughter leaves me, her mind filled with ideas and the barrow filled with everything she will need to fulfil them?

Not everything – Luke by Rother came yesterday before sunset and took the tools. I didn't see him. I should have liked to offer him some advice. However, the sight of his young body would have riled me as I pictured him digging the land. Meg knew this and she did right in not bringing him to me.

Anyway, Meg has gone to catch the incoming tide while I am stuck here waiting for Joan. She is a fine woman with soft brown eyes and gentle ways, so I must try... I will try... to show gratitude for her help.

Hell's teeth. I cannot reach the beaker of ale and what a fool I will look if Joan arrives to find I've toppled onto the floor. Only a saint could endure these coming weeks.

# Meg

What a day it has been. There have been moments when I've felt truly glorious to be a part of this great adventure and others when I have despaired to think of my father and his misery.

I rose at daybreak and left not long after, having tried not to show my frustration at the inevitable delays caused by the invalid's demands. With the barrow bumping along in front of me, I could not race as I wanted but kept a steady pace, my eyes darting from the ground to the group gathered at the water's edge.

Daniel wanted to leave at the first opportunity on the rising tide, taking advantage of the current which would help carry us towards our island. "The second journey will be trickier," he explained yesterday, "if the tide is on the turn, but we'll manage."

"And the third?" I had asked.

"Trickier still," he had admitted with a grin. "But we'll know it's our last. By then, the island will be surrounded by mud, and I'll need help with hauling the boat in."

Daniel was the first to spot me approaching and raised his arm in greeting before turning back to continue loading his boat. Eve and Sarah then stepped away from island-adventurers and curious well-wishers who had gathered to watch us leave. They joined me and lifted the front of my barrow, taking much of the weight, enabling it to be moved easily over ground which became increasingly stony and slippery as we neared the water. Excited chatter flew between us as they asked after my father, and we shared our anticipation and concerns about the coming days. As I reached the high tide line, I knew I had been accepted as part of the Middle Isle settlers.

"Leave the barrow there," Daniel called, "and your bag. They were placed by the pile of tools donated by my father.

"You'll be on the next trip," Sarah explained.

The first of the two boats was loaded with woollen sheeting and poles, then boxes and sacks with all the grain, fruit and vegetables to last us for at least a week. The second held two crates, each with four chickens, and sacks of clothing along with any personal belongings, a huge pan and a three-legged trivet. Amongst all of this, the first of the settlers balanced precariously on plank benches.

John Smithy had adopted the role of leader, and it was he who decided that the first job upon arrival would be to erect a tent and dig a fire-pit over which a pan of pottage would simmer as soon as the fire held a steady blaze.

"We'll need a spade and a pick," he called from the boat.

Luke, not much more than a boy but quick-thinking and eager, dashed over to me and asked, "Can I take yours?"

"They're here for everyone to use," I reassured him. Even the offering of the spade heightened my anticipation of our new life on the island.

With Daniel at the oars of his boat and his uncle taking charge of the second, they left our shore with John and Eve, Friar Matthew and Edwin Carpenter. The rest of us could only wait our turn as our gaze followed every rise and dip of the oars and the boats heading for Middle Isle.

The day was crisp, and the view of the island as clear as I had ever known it. But soon the boats and their passengers were no more than a low shape rolling up and down with the waves, and then we could no longer see them, however hard we strained our eyes. We could only guess if they had reached the shore and wondered if the boats slid against a sandy slope or a stony bank.

Soon we saw the boats returning and Sarah was saying that they must have barely stopped – just dropped off their load and turned back for us. With a grin, I found myself agreeing.

Before long, I was being ushered onto Daniel's boat, and he was passing rolls of blankets to be loaded at the far end. Then came my bag of clothes, and the sacks filled with seeds, peas and bulbs. Sarah sat beside me, a box of wooden plates and clay beakers on her lap, flasks of water at her feet.

We watched Luke at work in the second boat, as the tools, including John Smithy's and Edwin Carpenter's, were stacked along with several buckets and further rolls of blankets.

I heard Daniel saying that after this it would be just his boat on the third trip, filled with fishing kit, oak barrels, and his sack of clothes. The barrels, although empty, were bulky, yet essential to our plans to build a well. I hoped the currents would be kind to Daniel on that last journey of the day.

As we left, I thought of my father and how he should be the one sitting in the boat and me left at home with Joan as my companion. For a while, my enthusiasm was dampened as we headed north-east with our cloaks and shawls wrapped tight around us and our backs bent against the chill wind. In time, the view of Lydd had drifted into obscurity and the features of Middle Isle sharpened as it stretched out before us.

I had always suspected there to be a definite rise in the land. Now I saw it clearly to the right and imagined racing up the slope then turning back to see the whole of our island.

"Look at it!" I said to Sarah. "It's looking weary after the winter, but fresh growth is coming, and this land will be so green. Are those thorn trees? They must be – over there with the white blossom. The first signs of new life."

"They are!" she agreed. "And those tall trees... we'll be glad of their shelter."

"And their wood," Daniel commented from his position at the oars.

"What do you think the others are doing?" Sarah wondered. "Have they found the place to set up camp?"

"They must have. It must be done."

"I can see them!" Sarah tapped me on the arm before pointing to the figures heading towards the beach.

Grinning, I responded, "I can't wait to see it all."

The tide must have been at its highest when the boat crunched upon the shallow beach of sand and stones. Sarah and I scrambled out, helped by John and Edwin, while Daniel stayed onboard to hand over our belongings. Then the second boat was grinding to a halt on the shore and, in turn, we relieved it of its precious cargo of tools and rolls of blankets.

"We have decided on a place to set up home," John announced.

Home. He could have said camp or shelters. Home felt more permanent.

"We'll show you," Eve said, picking up a blanket roll and a sack of my seeds.

I slung a canvas bag over my shoulder and gathered two lots of the prized seeds in my arms, then looked helplessly at the stack of our belongings.

"We'll clear it in no time," John remarked, reading my mind, as he gathered tools. We paused briefly, turning to wave as best we could at the departing boats with Luke and Daniel at the oars.

Having never felt any warmth towards Daniel, it seemed odd to feel a sense of loss at his departure. In the space of a morning, we had become a Middle Isle family.

Now the six of us, as Luke had returned to Lydd and would then row back with Daniel, moved beyond the high tide mark and onto the raised area of rough grassland. At a glance, I could see that this ground was richer than the very best of our land between the Rype and the Rother. The grass grew thickly and promised to be lush once the days became warmer. I disturbed a bare patch with the toe of my shoe, revealing soil both rich and sticky brown, not like that at home – so sandy or full of stones that it scattered at my touch. Amory was right to set his sights on Middle Isle.

We had landed on the south-western end of the island, and I noted that the whole of it was about the same size as our town of Lydd and its common land, the Rype. Longer than it was wide, but with oaks, chestnuts and thorn bushes in the centre, whereas Lydd was mostly bare of trees. I knew that my father would have been satisfied to find the Isle so fertile and would recognise all the opportunities it offered. Silently, I vowed that if his leg were to mend sooner and better than anticipated, then Martin at Rype could come here to Middle Isle and be pleased with his daughter. He would find plots filled with a variety of healthy crops. Even now, having just stepped upon the land, I could picture it bursting with new growth.

"We can plan all this tomorrow," John said, gesturing to the open space. "Today we must prepare our shelter."

"I see the fire has been lit." I looked towards the trees and watched as a thin spiral of smoke filtered through the bare branches.

"Aye, and I must return to it. Vegetables are softening in the pan, but we need more water," Eve replied, eyeing the flasks of precious liquid resting on the ground. "John and Edwin have been digging a well, and we can only pray for fresh water rather than salty."

"It must be!" I felt an anxiety rise within me, forgetting about the bread and ale we carried with us – enough to sustain our small group for several days. "Or we'll be abandoning the island before we begin."

"We may be able to capture water from the river before it mixes with the sea," Friar Matthew, a man of few words, suggested. He was speaking of the Rother which flowed around the island, mixing with tidal waters.

"Ideal for washing, but probably not cooking," Eve suggested. "The men have made good progress and I feel certain we will be drawing water from our well within days. In the meantime, I am grateful for the flasks you have brought from Lydd, but we should use what we have sparingly."

"We *must* find fresh water," was all I could whisper to myself. "The well *must* go deep enough."

The landscape, at first open, became scrubby towards the centre of the island, with low lying bushes, for which I could see no use. We skirted this area and views towards Lydd were now shielded as we gazed across the far side of Middle Isle. The scrub became dominated by tall oaks and chestnuts, at least twelve of these fine trees, all in a slight hollow. I looked with pleasure at their strong trunks and sturdy branches. These were of great value to us, not only for shelter but for the fallen branches which littered the ground and would feed our fire for several months.

"We plan to clear this area." Already I could hear the pride in John's voice as he introduced Sarah and me to the copse we would call home. "It faces to the north-west, meaning we are saved from the icy winds from the north-east and the strong south-westerly gales. The first shelter can go here, and the second over there. You can see the fire, and the well is being dug over there, away from the tree roots."

By the time Daniel and Luke had returned and been introduced to our chosen space, an area had been cleared of dead branches and undergrowth. Hard ground and roots had been worked at until the ends of eight stout poles could be driven into the ground. Once secure, angled with their lengths leaning inwards, thinner poles were lashed to the frame. This created the structure to support our sheets of wool and shelter us overnight. A second tent would come but not immediately, John Smithy decided. The well had been dug to a depth of two feet, and twice as wide, but we had no expectations of reaching fresh water and shoring the sides for another day or two. It would take time to make our camp a home, and only when we had water and somewhere dry to sleep could we turn our attention to the land.

"Now we must eat!" Eve announced, taking her place by the pan of onions, turnips and carrots, the gravy thickened with barley.

Sarah, whose place was to assist Eve with the running of the camp, cooked flatbreads in a pan. I, who would mostly work on the land, handed out the plates of food then poured weak ale.

However satisfying it was to sit there, with the fire crackling and our shelter taking shape, I longed to fully explore the island. Only Friar Matthew lived by his own rules and, after we had eaten, he stood and declared, "We can none of us truly thank God for providing us with this sheltered hollow and our well which will flow with fresh water if we have no altar dedicated to His holiness."

The rest of us gazed towards the monk and waited for his next words. He had lived within our community in Lydd for four months, and we recognised him as a man who knew about the world beyond our small town. A knowledge of letters placed Friar Matthew in a position where the rest of us could only be in awe of his learning, and his personal channel to our Lord furthered our esteem.

"I shall seek out the place where He wishes me to place a cross to pledge our devotion."

With this, Friar Matthew left us to tend the fire, provide the next meal, and battle with the sheets of wool while we covered our shelter.

As I lifted the pot of hot water from the trivet and prepared to wipe the plates and beakers clean, I could not help but envy the monk as he left us and set off to the north-eastern and, as yet, unexplored, tip of the island.

# Jebediah of Romney

No one in the old port of Romney ever speaks of Middle Isle. Their fortunes come from the new town by the coast where ships dock, merchants trade, and a glorious church has risen by the beach. Sometimes they turn their attention inland, where the soil is rich and produce plentiful, and they feel blessed with this land.

No one living in Romney even bothers to look towards Middle Isle. It is nothing but a smudge on the landscape. An island squatting in the tidal waters of the Rother, surrounded by mud banks at low tide.

The island is my place and has been for the past five months.

I was born to a woman who was fair of skin. Memories of her golden hair and freckled nose still linger in my mind. Her voice flowed sweetly when she sang to me, but at times there came a sadness...

and tears. Her father, a spice merchant, sent me to sea when I was no more than nine years of age. I travelled to a place where the people looked more like me and less like my mother, but they were not my people, and I was glad to return to her. After my fourth voyage I helped unload the ship and, with small gifts in my shoulder bag, I set off at a brisk pace to the old port and my mother.

"She has gone," my grandfather told me.

"Dead?" I asked, a feeling of loss already weighing heavy upon me.

"Gone from here," he replied.

"Where shall I find her?"

"You will not. Go back to the boat. There is no home for you here."

And so, the boat became the only home I had as I travelled to places where people with dark skin and darker hair lived, and those people frowned at my pale brown skin. Then to Romney and along the coast to Winchelsea and Hastings where people with fair locks of hair glared at mine being dark even though I spoke their tongue as if I was one of them.

This journeying across the sea continued for years – perhaps twelve or more, until one day we moored at Romney, and I was too sick with the fever to help with the cargo. The captain, who had traded with my grandfather for years and earned his respect, left me with him and I slept in a stable for several days and nights until the sweating and fever passed. In this time, I saw nothing of my grandfather nor any other family, such as uncles or cousins who may have still lived locally. A manservant brought me weak ale, dry bread and bowls of broth with fish or meat. Sometimes there was cheese or sweet biscuits.

My strength returned and I took to walking well-worn trails by night, sometimes going inland but more often to the port from where my ship had departed while my fever was at its height. By day, I was no better than a prisoner in the stable. I waited and considered what I should do next.

Then one day my grandfather came to see me. Although I was now taller and stronger than the old man, I knew he still had a power over me. "You have the leprosy," he stated from the doorway of the stable. "Fortunately, there is a place for people like you. For lepers. The boy who feeds you will take you there, and they are expecting you. Be glad that they will take you."

I knew this to be a lie and probably the most wicked one ever to come from my grandfather's lips. There was no time to plan. I stuffed my blanket and shoes in a sack with my cloak, spare shift and stockings, then ran barefoot, past the wooden church to the water's edge. Thankfully, the tidal river was high, and I plunged into it, swimming underwater for several strokes then rising to the surface and, keeping an eye on Middle Isle, I ploughed onwards, slowly and steadily.

No doubt they thought I would have drowned. Hoped I had drowned. But I succeeded in reaching a place where I could live peacefully. Middle Isle is my island. No one else wanted it... Until today when the strangers came from Lydd.

Author's note: By the 12th century, there was a leper colony on the outskirts of New Romney. For the sake of the story, I have mentioned it here, knowing the dates do not fit.

# Meg

At last! At last I have been able to explore the whole of Middle Isle.

We went as a group, but not before the woollen sheeting was pulled taut and tied securely across the frame, making sure our shelter was ready for the coming night. And not before Sarah and I had gathered sack after sack of dry leaves from under the thorn trees, then spread them on the floor of the shelter to form a simple cushion between our blankets and the hard ground. And not before John and Luke had dug the well to a depth of four feet, and wider to give them space to work, so now they had to be hauled out, muddy but jubilant.

Friar Matthew has not been part of these endeavours to make our first days as comfortable as possible. Instead, he has seen to our spiritual needs and sought the best place to praise the Lord. When he led us from the camp to the highest point of the island, I wanted to run ahead, eager to see beyond the wooded area. But I held back, my gaze darting from the stretch of water between Midley and the old port of Romney, then towards Lydd.

In no time at all the ground had become curiously sandy and I nudged at it with the toes of my shoes. "But this is all sand and no earth at all," I said. "How can we...? How will we...? It is no use at all."

"You're right," John replied. "This is no good to us, but it is the only area with poor soil."

"He is right," Daniel insisted. "The land where the boat is beached may be stony, but it soon gives way to a good, brown earth and all the way from the beach to the camp, it looks to be fertile."

"And where we are digging the well, the earth is better than any I have ever seen in Lydd," Luke interrupted.

"This sandy ground is just at the nose of the island," Friar Matthew said. I liked the way he described it – the nose. It suited this raised place at the far north-east of Middle Isle.

We reached the summit, as I like to think of it, although in truth it is no more than a slight rise. From there I looked down at the beach of dark, golden sand curving around the end of the Isle, and the dangerous mudflats with their pools stretching towards the rising tide.

In the sky a blanket of dull grey obscured the sun, as I gazed towards the new port of Romney and the sea. Perhaps I could see a tall merchant ship riding at anchor in the deep part of the river, or perhaps it was a trick of the light as the waters shifted and I tried to focus. The town squatted there on the coast, close enough for me to have a hint of its existence, but too far to see any more than a dark smudge on the horizon. My eyes followed the river to the old port of Romney and I got a definite impression of properties. From there the river continued and I spotted a small ship sailing from some inland place to the coast, but everything else was indistinct. I turned back to our island in the estuary.

"This is the place where I shall thank God for his care of us while we live here." Friar Matthew pointed to the spot where he had lashed together two sticks to form a simple cross. "Edwin Carpenter, perhaps you could help me select wood and together we can create a cross more fitting for the purpose."

"Aye." Edwin nodded. "When we have shelter and fresh water."

The friar studied the sandy soil and continued, "Nowhere on this island will I find an altar stone worthy of Him, but I will look along the beaches and place the very best stone at the foot of the cross. Our community is new, and He will not judge us for our humble offerings. I will work alongside you on the land, and work as hard as any man, then will come here to show my devotion to Him. I will show my gratitude for this good soil and the shelter we have in the copse."

"Thank you, Brother, for coming with us," John Smithy responded. "You are a man of God, not of Lydd, and were free to go elsewhere but chose to come here and care for our souls. We are grateful."

The rest of us murmured our assent and we turned to continue our tour of the island. As we trailed around the edge of the Isle, I was relieved to see that the sandy nose soon gave way to brown soil. Silently, I reflected on the truth that without oxen, or any beast to help us, the task of breaking the earth and removing the tangle of roots, would be backbreaking, but satisfying.

Midway down the far side, we came across a shallow inlet with beaches of pebbles and sand, soon to be covered by the rising tide.

"This would be the perfect place to wash our pans and clothes," Eve commented. "If the fresh water still flows in here at low tide, and I believe it will, then perhaps we can collect it for cooking?"

We all gathered on the narrow beach and studied the grey water. I can picture, when the spring comes and we feel the warmth of the sun on our backs, Eve and Sarah pounding our clothes on the stones, releasing the soil embedded in the fibres. They will place the wet garments on the ground, or over the low bushes, taking care to turn them regularly. I will

65

be with the men, working the land into a condition where it is ready to nurture our crops. In places fresh, green shoots will be forging upwards, giving us satisfaction, and a knowledge that our hard work has been worthwhile.

My thoughts have wandered. I must return to our small group of settlers and our exploration of Middle Isle.

We continued walking around the island, noting how the shallow beaches soon gave way to brown soil. "There are some stones and shells in this earth but not too many," I observed. "It will break up easily with picks and spades. But there will not be so much of the salt-laden sand in it that our crops will struggle to find the goodness they need."

"Is it what your father hoped to find?" John asked.

"It is," I confirmed. "He said that the sea would have retreated leaving rich soil and he was right."

On reaching the other end of the island, we paused to watch the grey waters of the Rother advancing sluggishly and a flock of Sanderlings probing for worms in the shallow pools. Then we turned and picked up our pace, heading back to our camp. Now John led us through the centre of our land, across the area we planned to grow crops. On reaching the midway point, we skirted the thorn bushes and arching brambles.

"I'm keen to explore this place," Eve told us, and we all slowed a little. "There are treasures to be found here. Look! Rosehips – withered, I know, but if I can harvest enough then there may be some goodness to be found in them. Who knows what roots, berries and nuts can be found here."

"Middle Isle will serve us well," Friar Matthew reminded us. We all nodded our agreement.

"But that is for tomorrow," Eve said, referring to her searching for those treasures amongst the thorns.

"Aye, we have much to do and little time before sunset," John reminded us. He strode ahead saying, "I suggest three of us men work on the well – Daniel, Edwin and myself – while Friar Matthew and Luke check our shelter is secure for the night and gather firewood."

On our return, the camp appeared cluttered and disorderly. And no wonder because the one tent was scarcely big enough for the eight of us and our belongings once nightfall came. Tools lay heaped under a beech tree, while food hung in sacks from low branches. We had no stores, no hooks, no shelters, other than those provided by nature. I had been so caught up with the thrill of being on the island, but now felt the responsibility for my seeds, peas and onion bulbs.

We all bring our own skills and uses to this group and the island. Mine is to advise on when and where to plant our crops, but in the meantime, I must be sure to keep the seeds dry. Glancing towards Edwin Carpenter, a pick in hand and at work in the pit which is to become a well, I knew I could not ask him to make shelves or a cupboard to keep the damp and vermin at bay.

For a moment, I glanced over the ground, looking for the patches which appeared to have remained dry during recent rainfall, then my gaze lifted to the trees and the snug places between the branches where one of my sacks could rest away from any dampness in the soil.

"Eve," I began. "The men are busy, and I know a meal needs to be prepared, but my seeds must be kept dry. Can you spare me?"

Already putting scoops of flour into a bowl, Eve turned to me, "We all have our place here and yours is to tend the crops. That starts with the seeds. But this one tent," she nodded in the direction of the woollen sheets stretched over poles, "is intended for four, not eight. I'm not sure if anything else can be stuffed in it."

I glanced at a pile of long, straight stakes and bundles of cloth on top. "Tomorrow we will have two tents and it will be easier. The food must be kept dry too..."

"If Sarah gathers more dead leaves," Eve decided, "and there is plenty amongst the thorn bushes, then we will sleep all the better on a soft bed. You find a way of storing the seeds, I'll fill our bellies, and we'll all be satisfied with our work today."

My anxieties began to fade. "I have an idea..." I told her.

With a hand pick, I began to loosen the earth in a place where two thick roots surfaced and joined the trunk of a tall beech tree. Already a natural hollow, a large cavity was soon created. I cut the thinner roots with the knife I carried in a pouch hanging from my belt. Once satisfied with the depth of my pit, I took a bucket and a hand spade and headed for the tip of the island. Here I swiftly gathered golden sand, marvelling at how thick and pure it was, and returned to camp.

Back at the copse, Daniel stood inside the developing well, the ground now level with his waist. All three men looked to be satisfied with their progress. Hands and forearms were encrusted with earth and grins spread across their grubby faces. As I passed by, I heard John saying, "We're done for today. Let's wash at that creek before supper."

"A meal will never have been so welcome," Daniel replied.

Silently agreeing, I breathed in the tempting aroma of salted fish cooked in a broth flavoured by the remains of our earlier meal. Meanwhile, a fresh batch of flatbreads were being baked in a pan and piled on a wooden platter.

In the tent, I spotted movement and knew Sarah was emptying yet another sack of dry leaves on the hard earth. "When the men return, we will eat," she called through the opening.

"I'll be ready!" I glanced at the sun. Before long it would dip below the horizon, and by then we would be enjoying our meal around the glowing fire and sharing our thoughts about our first day in our new home.

Back at the beech tree, I tipped the sand into the hole and swifty levelled it. I took half of my sacks filled with seeds, peas and onion bulbs and placed them on the sand. Luke passed by with an armful of firewood. "Can you help?" I asked him. "I need to keep these dry and there is such little time before nightfall. Can you tie these, so they hang from this branch?" I pointed to the remaining sacks and then to a low branch. "I am putting some here and some underground. I have split them and will store them in these two places until I have somewhere better."

Dropping the firewood, Luke replied, "This can wait." Taking my length of thin rope and a sack, he immediately set about helping me.

When my father was unable to come to Middle Isle, Daniel by Rother did well to suggest his young cousin came. We have spent little time together, but he is cheerful and eager to work.

On my knees at the newly excavated store, I covered my collection of precious seeds, beans and bulbs with leaves and twigs, packing them down over and over. Luke and I carried his bundle of firewood the short distance to camp and followed the well-diggers to the creek. While the sun touched upon the horizon, I trod carefully on the unfamiliar ground and down the slope to the water's edge.

The icy water sent shivers rippling through my whole body, and I washed my hands quickly, picking dirt from under the nails. The men had abandoned their tunics and scrubbed up to their forearms – digging was a mucky task. In the dim light, I could only imagine how the earth must be clinging to the fabric of the tunics, but it was nothing that couldn't be brushed out in the morning. They were in high spirits, clearly pleased with their progress.

"First light, and we'll be lashing together a ladder," Daniel said as he removed his shoes. They had worked in bare legs, so now he stood in the shallows washing his calves.

"Will you reach water tomorrow?" I asked, scrambling up the bank and away from the creek.

"I'm sure we will, but it may be another day or two before the well is complete," he responded.

"We can't rush the job if we want clean water." Edwin joined Daniel, standing ankle deep and hurriedly attacking the grime.

"Water and shelter must come first," John stated. "Then the land. You've made a place to store the seeds, I hear."

They left the creek together and I waited while they fastened shoes and shook out their tunics before replacing them. With our labouring finished for the day, it was a time to don thick cloaks and settle around the fireside, but for now we rubbed our arms and stamped our feet to bring warmth to our limbs as we walked back to camp. Behind us, the last of the yellow streaks across the grey sky faded. With the moon obscured by low cloud, nightfall came early on our first evening as settlers on Middle Isle.

# Jebediah

I cannot hide from these people who have arrived on my island. There are eight of them, but to me they are a swarm. They will be here and there – scavenging for the last of the berries and seeds, using my creek for fresh water and gathering firewood from the copse. By day, it will be near impossible for me to move about without being spotted.

It seems apparent that they plan to stay for some time. There is even a monk who has put a crude cross on the highest part of the land. He ventured close to my hide, and I feared he would discover me, but he didn't. Not this time. Whereas they have built a tent, my home is a hollow dug in the sand with a roof of curving wooden planks, part of a wrecked boat.

Now they sit around a fire, and I hear their voices drift towards me. Amongst the rise and fall of their chatter, laughter often breaks out. These people must be happy to be on Middle Isle – their voices are not those of people banished from their homes. I cannot help but wonder what brings them here.

The aroma of food causes my hollow stomach to twist and turn, and their fire burns bright. Mine is nothing more than a pile of ash under a clod of turf. Hopefully the embers will glow when I add dry bark and twigs. To be without fire would bring misery to my time here, especially during these early spring days when I am chilled to the bone all the time that I am not moving about. I have decided to let my kindling come to life now they have settled and can only hope they do not notice my ribbon of smoke. The flames will be deep within their pit.

All day my thoughts have been thrown about from one extreme to the other. No wonder my mind has been lively, when all I could do was remain hidden in my humble shelter, my cloak wrapped tight around me. One moment I am convinced that I must steal their boat and leave this island, for we cannot live together without me being discovered. The next, I wonder if they would welcome me as part of their... their family. If we could live together in harmony. Foolish thoughts. Why would these people be any different to those living in the old port at Romney?

Now, as I stand watching them, my whole being is filled with a loneliness not felt over the past months, and I know my choice must be made before dawn.

# Meg

The strangest thing happened this morning, the first of many waking on Middle Isle. We thought we were alone on the island. No one ever said... No one ever thought that someone might have been here before us. Now, instead of my thoughts being filled with tilling the land or making our shelter more comfortable, all I think of is Jebediah who came into my life this very day.

While we all gathered around the fire and spoke of our plans, empty bowls of porridge on our knees, he must have been waiting for the right moment to approach us. The first we knew of him was when he spoke, "Greetings!" A cough followed and he raised his voice a little: "Fair morn, newcomers to Middle Isle. I come in friendship and am alone." We all turned towards him, each one of us stunned into silence.

The stranger spread his arms, showing the pale pink of his palms and that he held no weapons. He smiled a smile that extended warmth and friendship towards us. The pale brown skin creased at the sides of his eyes, and his upturned mouth revealed teeth so white and even. As we stood there in awe, he ran his hand through his mop of almost-black tumbling curls and declared, "I have been here all winter and before. Since the autumn solstice."

John Smithy rose, then Edwin and Daniel. The rest of us waited.

"We have come from Lydd," John said. "And we thank you for your welcome."

I felt the tension leave my body. Turning to Eve, I looked for guidance.  She stood, as did Sarah. They raised their hands to greet this newcomer to our camp, and I found myself reacting in the same way. Now surrounding him, several of us were asking questions, but the poor man could not answer them. Too many came at once.

"I have not spoken to anyone all through the winter," he admitted. "I did not expect to see anyone again. Not since I left Romney."

And so we learned a little more about him.

"Where do you come from?" John asked. "You speak in our tongue, but where...?"

"Romney. I come from the old port of Romney, although I have been at sea for many years."

I frowned, not understanding. *He looks like he comes from a faraway land – from one of the places where the spices and silks originate. Does he mean...*

*does he mean that by being in those lands he has changed and now he looks as if...*

"My mother died when I was away at sea," he told us. "She was from a Romney family, her father being a merchant in the old port. I am Jebediah of Romney, but my father... my father I know nothing about him. He was not a man of Romney nor from the Kingdoms of Kent or Sussex. He came from across the seas and that is all I know. I have no home in Romney now and so I came here..."

*His story is complicated. Too much to reveal at this moment,* I realised.

"Were you stranded? Have you lost a boat?" John asked.

"Nay, I came by choice." Jeb faltered, clearly unsure of himself. "I came by choice," he repeated. "But I would have preferred to have been made welcome across the water there." He looked in the direction of the old port at Romney. "I am making this place my home, at least for a while."

"You've had troubles," Eve said. "And did not expect to have to explain yourself to strangers. You have told us enough. Perhaps in time..."

"Thank you." Jebediah smiled once more. "You are right, I did not expect..." His words faded.

"I'm sorry you are alone," John said. "Have we interrupted your peace? We plan to settle here for some time."

"I'm glad to see new faces," Jebediah replied. "But what brings you to this lonely isle?"

"We are here to farm the land."

"That is a worthy reason and I wish you luck." Jebediah paused as if uncertain how to voice his next words. "I wish I had your skills, but if I can help..."

"Would you like to work the land, Jebediah of Romney?" John asked. "Can you break up the soil until it crumbles? Can you gather and chop wood for our fires? Or gather reeds to thatch the roofs of the homes we will make?"

"There is no need for these things on a ship," he replied. "But I am young and strong and willing."

"Then I will call you Jebediah of Middle Isle," John stated, "and would welcome your help. Work alongside us and we will gladly share our meals with you."

"You know this island, and we did not come to make enemies." Edwin gestured for Jebediah to sit on one of the logs we were using as a bench at the fireside.

"I thank you for your welcome." Jebediah sat and accepted the beaker of ale offered by Eve.

"But we did come to work," Daniel pointed out. "The days are still short, and our tasks are many."

The murmurings of welcome towards Jebediah ceased, if only for a moment, while each one of us was left to ponder Daniel's words. The others may have been silently agreeing with the truth in his comments – we *are* here to work and there *is* much to be done. But I was wondering if Daniel by Rother had taken an instant dislike to this man who had come amongst our family of settlers. If Jebediah were indeed willing to live and work alongside us, everything would shift a little within our group, perhaps altering the plans we had made. My thoughts then drifted to the home he had already made on this land and how he had fended for himself. I wondered if he was happy in his solitude, not wanting nor expecting to join us.

"Daniel is right." John smiled at Jebediah, and we all knew that the offer of friendship had not been withdrawn. "We have been making our plans for the day, and work beckons."

"Then I'll work with you now, so you have not been hindered by my arrival."

As our thoughts turned to our various tasks, we were left not knowing how Jebediah came to be on Middle Isle. There was a story to be told, but no time for us to hear it.

Daniel gestured to Luke, and they stepped away from the group, collecting their picks and shovels before turning to the well. Edwin followed, as it had already been agreed who would work on each job.

"Will you join us for our midday meal?" John continued. "We would like to know about your time here. How you eat and where you find fresh water."

"Thank you. I will," Jebediah responded. "But before that I will help in any way I can. I have become unused to company but would welcome it."

As the sun rose in the sky and the low-lying clouds dispersed, we all set about our labours.

I have been so full of thoughts of Jebediah, or Jeb as he has asked us to call him, that I have made no mention of our first night under the woollen sheeting of our tent. We three women slept at the far end, with the men butted up against our feet and close to the opening. Our bed of leaves seemed comfortable at first, but I woke several times to feel every stone and protruding tree root. With barely enough space for the eight of us it was unpleasant to be so close. I think we were all awake before dawn when Friar Matthew took the opportunity to creep out, leaving the copse for his holy place.

With Jeb made welcome, and knowing he was eager to help, he was set to work. Alongside John, he dug holes in the hard ground, and I helped to hold the poles in place while they fastened them together to create the framework for a second tent. As we worked, John spoke of us making a more permanent shelter later, and we discussed our plans for growing crops. The men discarded their cloaks. I found myself intrigued by the brown colour of Jeb's skin and had an unexpected urge to reach out and touch his forearms. John's arms were pale and covered in wiry dark hairs, while Jeb's were almost free of hair. I wondered if, when the summer sun beat down on us, he would cast aside his tunic and would his chest and back be as smooth as his arms?

Will he still be with us when the summer comes? I hope so.

The growing heaps of earth around the tents and well led John's talk to return to making better shelters over the coming months. We discussed mixing straw from the reedbeds with earth and packing it into a framework of wood. This work will keep Edwin Carpenter busy, but there are enough men to labour on the land and every one of us will be glad of a solid home.

"Or Edwin may prefer to make walls from planks cut from fallen trees," John suggested. "No doubt he'll know what's best."

For now, two tents will shelter us. Sarah gathered more dry leaves, hauling sacksful back to camp, and I went to help her.

"He has a fine figure," she whispered to me as we tipped the leaves into piles at the far end of the new tent.

I blushed to think of Jebediah stretching the sheeting into place and said nothing in response. If I had reached out, I could have touched him through the woollen sheeting. *What sort of place does he live in?* I wondered. *What sort of place that meant he remained hidden from us yesterday? I would like to see it.*

By midday, three rolls of bedding had been moved from our first tent to the second. The women will share one tent and the men the other. As I watched Friar Matthew dragging lengths of fallen branches to a growing pile of firewood, I wondered if he minded sharing. *Perhaps he would prefer to be alone? Perhaps, in time, he will have his own shelter.*

Eve and I began organising our tent. Setting the now empty chicken crates on their sides, we decided to use them as store cupboards for food. We piled the plates and pans on the ground, there being no other place for them, and we still couldn't ask Edwin to make us shelves, not while he was so busy. To keep our cloaks from the damp ground we created hooks by lashing small lengths of timber to the tent frame.

"Do you think he wants to live here with us?" Sarah asked, once more referring to Jeb.

"We'll find out soon enough," Eve replied.

I said nothing, but I wondered... I wondered what it would be like to lie with Jeb of Middle Isle beside me through the night.

There came a cheer from the direction of the well, and I hurried to the doorway in time to see Edwin being helped up from its depths.

"They've done a fine job," Eve commented. "I have a feeling we'll have fresh water before long."

We watched as they left the shelter of our copse and headed towards the creek to wash the muck from their hands and arms. Curious, I wandered towards the pit and peered in. It was deep, deeper than I had expected, with a ladder of young branches lashed together.

My eyes adjusted to the darkness and I could see a small pool of water emerging. The success of the well was vital to our staying on Middle Isle. Stepping back, I gazed at the men. Daniel turned and gave a wave. I raised my hand in response, but movement behind diverted my attention. As Jeb approached, I wondered where he had discovered fresh water for his own use over the last months but found myself lost for words.

# Daniel

It seemed as if the eight of us on Middle Isle had formed a firm friendship. Each person is determined to make a success of our time here. But now someone else has arrived. He came this very morning. I don't know what skills Jebediah of Romney will bring. He says he was a sailor, so why is he not on a ship bound for some other place? Why has he been living here in hiding? Man is not meant to live alone.

I see the way Meg admires him, and for no good reason. His shoulders are no broader than mine, his legs are no longer than mine and his back no straighter.

Jebediah of Romney is a man who carries secrets. Women are not impressed by this. Women like to know who a man is and where he hails from. At least that is my belief.

# Meg

How our camp has changed within a day of us being on Middle Isle. As I lie on my mattress of dry leaves at the end of the second day, I cannot feel the tree roots and stones beneath me anymore, and my blankets nestle snug against me. Sarah and Eve are sleeping on either side, while the rest of the tent is to be used for storing food, eating and cooking implements.

The men are nearby but there has been talk of Friar Matthew having his own shelter, or cell as he calls it. This will take time, John says. Tomorrow we will start working on the land and that is our priority.

Jeb has his hidden den, not far from the friar's holy cross. We learnt more about him while eating and resting at the fireside. He is content to remain in his own place, to fish and forage, but will happily work with us on the land. I think he prefers to work alongside us but is reluctant to press himself upon our small group.

"He is a man who has lived amongst men on a ship," Sarah has commented. "He is used to company, and I think he welcomes us being here. But why is he on this island?"

Sarah voices her thoughts where I choose to keep mine to myself.

"He will tell us when he is ready," I say.

No one has mentioned that Jeb's skin is darker than ours, his hair a thick glossy brown, and his eyes almost black. He told us that his dead mother was the daughter of a merchant from Romney and his father unknown to him. I think his father is the reason for Jebediah being so dark. He and I have something in common – we have both lost our mothers. Perhaps I will tell him. Maybe tomorrow.

There is one person who appears to be wary of Jebediah. I have noticed Daniel watching him and he does not smile or talk with him as the other men do. Since my father had his accident, I have warmed to Daniel and now I am unsure of him again. If he has taken against Jeb, then I hope he does not persuade his cousin Luke to think as he does.

Once again my thoughts wander to the newcomer, but we are here to make a settlement and to farm the land.

Today, the ladder was extended, until one of the men stood about ten feet below ground level, digging and filling a bucket which was then hauled up by the other two. When it came to the point that Luke stood up to his knees in rising water, they decided it was time to stop. We women had already combed the beaches looking for clean pebbles and these were thrown into the pit. When the well bucket knocks against the base of the well, silt will not rise and muddy our water. Then we all watched as two of the barrels, those awkward things which took up so much space on the boat, were lowered into the pit. The two had already been fastened together but Edwin worried about the awkwardness of joining the next one when there was so little space around it.

Although the pit was excavated to be wide enough to work in and then refilled around the edges, Edwin had been right. While Sarah and I made the second tent into a comfortable shelter and store place, we sensed the well-diggers were becoming frustrated.

"Sarah, come and help," Edwin called for his wife. "Your hands are smaller than ours."

Edwin is a man with wide shoulders and fists like wooden mallets, whereas Sarah is slim, like a willow sapling, with long, tapering fingers. She smiled, and said to me, "Would you mind?"

"Of course not."

Edwin climbed up the ladder, out of the well pit, and Sarah replaced him. I couldn't hear their words, but he was obviously explaining how the third barrel was to be attached to the second, and she managed to manoeuvre a tool so plates could be fixed in place.

A cheer came from the three men, as Sarah clambered out. By then I had moved to the fireside. While flatbreads browned in the pan, there came a rhythmic thud of earth being shovelled back into the gap between the outer side of the barrels and the edge of the hole. When the men gathered for supper, they were jubilant – the first inches of fresh water were settling within the walls of the oak barrels.

At dusk, we all trailed after Friar Matthew to the rise on Middle Isle and stood in silence while he thanked the Lord for the clean, clear water, the fair weather which had allowed us to work unhindered, and the fish caught in Daniel's net. Sarah and John carried clay pots with tallow candles and, as I focussed on the flickering flames, my world became enchanted. The friar's voice rose and fell, his tone melodic, and I felt a warmth spread over me, my heart filling with love for this new settlement we are creating and the people who I live with as if we are one family.

My thoughts wandered to Jeb and his mother leaving him alone in this world, and then to Father and our home across the water. For the first time, I grieved for the brothers or sisters who had died in the years following my birth, and the lost chance of being part of a larger family when growing up.

Friar Matthew's voice rose, and my attention returned to the moment as those around me murmured their thanks and joined the monk in his final prayer.

Darkness had wrapped itself around Middle Isle, and our pace was slow as we walked back to the camp in the copse, the ground underfoot being unfamiliar. In time Friar Matthew will beat a track to his wooden cross while he travels to and fro to offer his devotions, but as yet there is no path, and we must tread carefully.

Jebediah did not return with us, and I didn't notice him leave. Perhaps tomorrow I will learn where he lives.

# Meg

Today, our third on Middle Isle, we fell easily into our planned roles. Although there was still so much to do in our camp, the land beckoned me, and I felt glad about John's eagerness to start work on it.

Edwin and Luke continued filling the void between the barrels and outer edge of the well. After that other plans are in place (and how exciting this is to think about). Edwin will start making ploughs. There will be two of them and as we have no beasts and no way of bringing them here, we shall pull the ploughs ourselves. However, Edwin's main role over the coming weeks is to create a frame for a long, low house and provide a more robust home for us. John has assured him that he will always have another man to work alongside him.

I have jumped forward again and must return to today. As soon as we had broken our fast, John, Friar Matthew and I set off to survey the land, carrying long-handled picks and spades. Gripping the smooth wooden handle of a pick, I could hardly keep the grin off my face. I knew that we were not just inspecting the ground but would begin the long and arduous task of preparing it for the seeds.

Daniel joined us, having first checked on his boat. Then we all stood beyond the copse and the scrubby thorn bushes, gazing at the land gently undulating towards the south-west. Before any plans had been made, we were alerted to someone else approaching and all turned to see Jebediah striding towards us.

"Good day!" John called out to Jeb, with the rest of us echoing his words.

While greetings were exchanged, I noted that within the short time I had known Jeb, his back had straightened and his smile had become more relaxed.

"How was it?" Jeb asked. "Your second night here."

"More comfortable for having two tents," John told him.

"And the well?"

"We have fresh water!" Friar Matthew told him.

"But our priority is the land," Daniel pointed out, once more seeming to be irritated by Jeb.

"How can I help?" Jeb asked.

"This land needs clearing," John indicated the ground before us. "We need to mark out two, perhaps three, strips and prepare it for crops. We have no beasts, as you know, just us who you have already met here on the Isle."

"We have good tools," Friar Matthew offered.

"And passion!" Jeb added.

"I'm glad of your help," John said to Jeb. "Look at this unbroken land… this unploughed land… we need strong young men and have one here in you."

Middle Isle seems to fit neatly into two halves. From Lydd, I had always imagined it to be oval and that is how it is, with the furthest end pointing towards the old port of Romney. Taller, upright trees come next. Not many of them, perhaps twelve or fifteen, but enough to offer us firewood and shelter, as well as the wood needed to make a solid home. If Middle Isle is to become a permanent settlement, then the woodland must be managed as it is precious to us. This is what Edwin says and he is right. He has spotted some trees that can be coppiced and will grow new shoots to benefit us in the years ahead. In the centre, those thorny bushes, threaded with brambles and roses, grow low and bow with the south-westerly winds. It is here, at their bases, that Sarah gathered the leaves for our beds. Eve speaks of the treasures to be found in the form of rosehips, berries and sloes.

The unbroken land which John spoke of makes up half the island. It is the area we saw most clearly from Lydd and the place where we landed and hauled the boats onto the beach. On the other side, beyond the copse, there is more good soil before it gives way to the rise of golden sand where the friar has placed his cross. This is where Jeb lives, and I wonder why he chose that place and not to sleep under the shelter of the trees.

John decided to pace out three plots, leaving wide paths between each.

"Daniel, Jeb and I have much the same length of stride," he observed. "Daniel, if you start there and measure twenty-two yards across, then Friar Matthew can mark the corners with stones or whatever comes to hand. Meg, you will do the same. Look about the place and gather anything we can use to mark the corners of our plots."

"Are they to be an acre?" Daniel asked.

John looked at me and I considered the length of 220 strides, or yards. It was too much. Too much for now.

"Half an acre would be more manageable," I suggested. "110 strides."

"That is for the best," John replied. "Let's not make our task near impossible. Three half- acre plots would be a fine start."

So we began, with Daniel measuring the width of the first plot then, as he started on the length, Jeb began his strides for the next plot. The grass was thick, and it soon became apparent that striding was easier than finding enough stones as markers. Instead, the Friar and I retreated to the thorn bushes and cut branches then pressed the severed ends into the earth. It took some time before we all returned to the spot where we had first stood to make our plans.

"All this work and not one clod of earth has been turned," John observed. "Let's quench our thirst and come back. If there has been good progress with the well, then Luke must join us here when Daniel goes to fish."

On our return, both Sarah and Luke joined us. The men began to dig clods of earth, thick with grass roots, while Sarah and I lifted them, shook off the loose soil and placed them along the borders of our plots. It soon became apparent that the waste would need moving elsewhere. Before long we would be debating how this waste could be used for our benefit. As we toiled, I imagined that however weary we felt, however much our bodies ached, our evening talk around the fireside would be lively as new plans and ideas were discussed.

By the time we returned to labour after our midday meal, Daniel had joined us again. Fishing just for our meals, meant his time in the boat was short. Luke had returned to work alongside Edwin, and Friar Matthew to his cross. This is how it will be on Middle Isle – people will move from one task to another.

The afternoon's task was both exciting and disheartening. Working two plots at the same time meant little progress was made. In Lydd the ground is stoney, the earth light and sandy, meaning land can be cleared quickly. Other areas are reclaimed from the banks of the retreating Rother, and they are mostly free of roots and weeds. But here each foot of land made ready for the plough is a hard-won battle. Yet having removed the top surface, we find good brown earth with a scattering of beach pebbles and shells which tells the story of a time before Middle Isle rose from the tidal waters. Although tempted to dig through this, turning it and breaking up the clods, we resist and continue to remove the top layer which cannot be used for planting crops. The underlying earth will be lifted with the plough Edwin is already crafting. Rounded pebbles and rough shells offer drainage and stop it from becoming too heavy. This soil on Middle Isle is just as my father imagined.

"Meg!" Daniel called as we worked together on a plot.

"Aye?" I turned, a clump of soil and matted grass heavy in my arms.

"Will your father be pleased?"

"He will." I dropped my armful with the others. "You'll be able to send a message? When you return in a few days?"

"I will," Daniel replied. "And one day he'll be here to see it for himself."

We worked well – Daniel, Luke and I – on the first strip of land, with John, Jeb and Sarah toiling on the second. By the time the light was fading, each plot had been cleared along its width and to a length of about three yards. Cleaning our boots on tufts of grass, we made our way to the creek to wash. Fortunately, the aprons we were wearing prevented our tunics from becoming too heavily soiled, but our exposed hands and arms were caked in mud.

We paddled ankle deep in the cold water, our feet sinking into the sand. "There's a lot of seaweed in places," Daniel remarked. "Where the tide brings it in, you know."

"We should gather it when we can," I replied. He must have known it was good for the soil, rich in nutrients.

Since Jebediah had joined us on the island, I had felt some of my unreasonable ill-feeling towards Daniel return. But the afternoon spent working together had pushed it aside. He had laboured as hard as any of us, but more importantly to me, he had thought about Father and his plans for Middle Isle. Daniel had proven himself to be a good friend.

However, while we leaned down to wash our hands and arms in the chilly water, I found myself standing next to Jeb.

"What brought you here?" he asked. "To Middle Isle."

"It was my father," I began. "He was meant to be here…"

"Meg! Use this patch of clean apron," Daniel interrupted. "Your hands will soon become sore if they are left wet."

He meant well. At least I think he did, because he was right. We must care for ourselves as best we can as we didn't come equipped with all the salves and lotions that would be to hand if we were back in Lydd. But I can't help wondering if Daniel wanted to prevent me from speaking with Jeb, and I can't help thinking how I would have liked to walk back to camp with Jeb at my side. But instead, it was Daniel who fell in step beside me.

# Meg

This evening, at sunset on the end of our fourth day on Middle Isle, we relaxed at the fireside, and John told us Jeb's story.

"We've been talking, me and Jeb, while we worked on the land today," he said. "We all know that he's from over the water at Romney, but not what brought him here. It was the grandfather, his only relative, who drove him away. Jeb was at sea, as he said. He travelled from place to place and once he learnt his mother was gone, he never returned to his grandfather. He always stayed on the boat. Until recently.

"He was sick, you see. Too sick to stay on the boat, so he went to his grandfather. The old man looked after him, or at least his manservant did. But then the grandfather did a terrible thing – he wanted to be rid of Jeb, so he said he was sending him to the leper colony down the river at the new port of Romney."

We all listened, at first fascinated by this story, and then horrified.

"We have a man amongst us with leprosy?" Daniel barked.

"What will become of us?" Sarah whimpered.

"We have a man whose grandfather attempted to be rid of him and created a terrible lie," John stated. "Jebediah is as healthy as any of us."

"There must be some truth in it," Daniel insisted. "Some symptoms... some reason for it."

"The only truth is that a man in the old port has a cruel and ruthless streak," John replied. "Jeb came here to live in peace. He has told me his story and asked me to tell you all, so there is no mystery as to why he's here. He came to hide from his grandfather. So now you know and there is no more to say about it."

"Only that every day Jebediah works hard on the land and him being here can only be good for us," Edwin added.

"And you're sure..." Sarah's voice was high, her words rushed.

Edwin took one of her hands in his. "If John has heard Jeb's story and believes him then that's good enough for me."

"Of course," she murmured.

"Jeb knows that we all need to understand what brought him here," John continued, "and I ask that he be left to work alongside us without having to speak of what happened over the days leading up to him coming to Middle Isle."

I said nothing, but sat with my cloak wrapped tight around me, my gaze fixed on the solid glow of the embers and the youthful flames darting about the firewood. Glad to know Jeb's story, my determination to help him feel at ease within our community grew.

"It makes no sense to me," Daniel persisted. "There must be some reason…"

# Jebediah

There are three women living here on Middle Isle. Eve is the wife of John, who they sometimes call John Smithy, although he has no forge here yet. She is gentle and kindly, asking if I am comfortable and ready to reassure me that I am welcome to eat with them. This evening, while we ate, Eve spoke of preparing soothing ointments to rub into our chafed hands. She plans to forage for plants to make remedies. I see her as someone who would be ready to come to the aid of anyone suffering from a minor injury or illness. John Smithy is the leader as he is the most elderly of the menfolk, although there is talk of another man – Martin, they call him – and how he was meant to be here.

The second woman is Sarah, a young woman married to Edwin Carpenter. She is quick to smile, and laughter often bursts from her. Whereas Eve reigns over the meal preparation and camp, Sarah is sometimes there, sometimes in the fields, and I believe she will work wherever she is most needed.

The third is Meg. At times I thought her to be married to Daniel the fisherman, but she wears her hair loose, so is not yet wed. Perhaps there is an agreement between them, as he seems to watch over her and rushes to her side whenever possible. Or perhaps he wishes there to be love between them and she knows nothing of it. Meg is excited to be here. I see it in her eyes which gleam when she talks about preparing the land for planting and the seeds which will flourish. She is eager to work on the land, however hard it is. We have barely spoken but I feel that every day when Meg wakes, she is joyful about the new opportunities and the tasks to be completed that day.

I hope she never wakes beside Daniel.

# *John Smithy*

When we follow the monk to his cross – or is it our cross? – I thank the saints for many things. I am not a man of words. I am a man of action. If I speak of one thing before the other, it does not mean I put more weight on it.

The weather has been mild since our arrival on Middle Isle, meaning we could set up our beds under the woollen sheeting and gather leaves for our mattresses without the wind whipping them about or the rain hindering us. Wood for the fire has been gathered and stacked. While we dig and remove clod after clod of earth and grass, the sun shines, albeit weakly, upon us. It is back-breaking work and seems as if it will be never-ending, so I am grateful for the bright days and thank Saint Medard, knowing we are in his care. In a month or so, after the first seeds are sown and the first tender shoots appear, Saint Medard will be in our thoughts and prayers to him on our lips. He is the patron saint of both weather and agriculture.

My wife Eve, mother to our boys, is steadfast and devoted to our own family and the family here at Middle Isle. She has become a mother to them all. I thank Saint Monica for my good wife.

Before our arrival, Jeb collected rainwater, in dishes carved from fallen branches, and from puddles. We need a well and I thank Saint Marina for the clear water rising in our well.

"My needs are simple," the monk said to me this evening, after our devotions at the cross. "I cannot expect Edwin to be spared to make a cross more befitting for our Lord, and I am happy to praise Him while working on the land, rather than leave our work to come here and pray."

But he wanted something from those of us on Middle Isle who had so little.

"A stone altar would be... Just a piece of stone."

"There is no stone here!" I replied. How did he think we could hew stone from earth, shingle and sand?

"There is!" His words rang out. "I prayed for an altar stone, and it came to me!"

I glanced back to the cross, half expecting an altar to have appeared. But dusk had wrapped itself around the Isle and we were walking back to the copse. There was nothing to be seen.

"Came to you?" I queried.

"A limestone slab has washed up on the beach! It is not too big. Not too big for two young men and me to carry up there." He gestured towards the rise on the land where we prayed.

With reluctance, I have agreed that Friar Matthew can take Daniel and Luke from the field tomorrow morning so he can have his stone. I wonder how Martin at Rype would have responded to this request. He is a man who knows about the land, but does he know about people? Friar Matthew will work all the harder for being allowed to have his altar stone.

# Meg

Seven days have passed since we came to Middle Isle. Today, after our midday meal, Daniel left us to sail back to Lydd for the first time since we arrived. There are supplies to be collected and news to be passed on. As I relax at the fireside, my stomach comfortably full of pottage, I think about him reaching the beach in Lydd and the news he will be eager to share.

The morning's work has been satisfying, although tiring. My body aches, but it is too soon for me to leave our island, if only for a short time. I'm keen to be a part of clearing the land and must press on with it, as I told John earlier.

"Meg, would you like to go with Daniel?" John asked as we met on the pathway between the plots. "You could see your father." We were both dumping a heavy clod, and I was about to turn away when he spoke. I don't like to break my rhythm of lift, carry, drop, turn.

"Thank you, but he knows I must work. He expects me to work." With this I trudged back to Luke, passing Jeb as I went.

We were labouring in two groups, each clearing one plot. In the first, Luke dug while Jeb and I carried. Half the land was now clear of grass, weeds and roots, with much of the bare earth flattened by our constant trudging back and forth.

"What makes you smile?" Luke asked as he passed the next clod to me.

"We have cleared more than half, and I am picturing it with the earth turned by Edwin's plough," I replied, moving away before he could respond.

Propped against the straight trunk of a beech tree in the copse, the new plough waited to be used. Thankfully, John Smithy had thought to bring recently crafted blades with him.

Once more I walked towards the pathway, passing Jeb, meeting John as we both dropped heavy clods, passing Jeb once more.

"Two more days and this plot will be ready for the plough," Luke commented on my return.

"Aye!" I grinned.

Jeb started clearing the pathway, moving the clods, and so when he returned, the pattern of us walking to and fro had changed. Now we were side-by-side. "Did you keep dry last night?" he asked. "The rain came down hard, and I wondered how you all fared."

"We kept dry," I told him. "It helps to be sheltered by the trees, and I wasn't disturbed by the rain."

That was true enough. I usually slept without waking. However, something else had disturbed us. Edwin had come to our tent to lie with his wife.

I didn't want to think about the grunts and moans. This is how a child begins to grow. My father was right to think a baby is likely to be born to our Middle Isle family.

"How do you shelter?" I asked.

"Soon after I arrived, I dug a hole in the sand then used the wood from a boat for the roof. It is no more than a pit, but I stay warm and dry."

"A boat?" I asked. I have been curious about his home since he walked into our camp. He works with us all day and eats with us but always goes back to his own shelter after nightfall. I know he returns occasionally during the day to tend a fire, to make sure it is smouldering, but otherwise he is with us.

When Eve, Sarah and I go to our tent at night, I find myself glancing back and I see the smoke from his fire. What does Jebediah think about when he is alone? Does he think of the places he has been and the people he has met? Is he lonely? He is a stranger to me still, and wary of us, but I sense that he wants to be friends.

"Not a whole one," Jeb explained. "Not enough to use on the water, but enough for my roof. It was washed up on the beach over there." He gestured to the north-west, near to where we worked.

I pondered on the valuable wood found on the beach. We came to Middle Isle with boatloads of belongings and the opportunity of returning to Lydd for food and anything else we needed... anything else that fitted in Daniel's boat. How different it was for Jeb.

"There was a fleece on the beach once!" he told me later as we continued to clear the land. "I'm going to pull at it, bit by bit, to make it into a workable yarn and then I'm thinking of weaving it to make a thick cloth. By the autumn, I'll have a cloak!"

"I'm glad you found useful things," I said. "Glad you survived the winter."

We continued. Lift, carry, drop, turn.

"You can come and see it," Jeb suggested after a while. "The boat. The wool. If you like?"

"I'd like that." My response was restrained but inside I glowed.

After a while Jeb and Luke swapped roles. The rhythm changed, and now I passed Luke rather than walk alongside Jeb. On the other plot they had swapped too, and I met Daniel at the path.

"He's not one of us," Daniel said to me, interrupting my thoughts of emerging seedlings and sunnier days.

"Who?" I responded, feeling lost for a moment.

"Jeb. Who is he? We know so little about him."

Visions of neatly furrowed land vanished and I returned to the present. "We know he works hard and wants to be our friend. We know he has spoken to John about his life, and John has shared it with us."

"Don't be too friendly, Meg. Your father wouldn't like it."

"You can't know that, Daniel. You can't know what my father would think." I scowled. "Father thinks of us growing crops and if there is another man to help, he will be happy enough."

"This man has dark skin like the men who bring spices, materials and wine. How can he know about growing crops?"

I knew Daniel didn't like Jeb. I had sensed it from the start, but I hadn't expected this to be thrown at me – for him to be so direct in revealing his true thoughts.

"Don't you like those men?" I asked.

"I like them well enough when they come and go. I wouldn't like them to stay," he replied. "They have their own place."

"But Jeb lives here now. He has no other place."

Daniel's words confused and annoyed me. Had he not heard Jeb's story? Did he not want to believe that Jeb came from the old port of Romney – just over there... just across the water?

"I have work to do," I replied. "Work to finish before we eat."

Not long after, as we tucked into thick broth, I made sure to avoid Daniel.

Now he has left for Lydd, carrying tales of our first week on Middle Isle, and will return with ale and winter vegetables. I worry what other stories or gossip he will tell.

# Meg

In just a week our Middle Isle family is almost destroyed. I had sensed a hint of the trouble to come in the way Daniel spoke about Jebediah. Although I never thought... never imagined that it would be any more than a grumble from him. We came to the island with the intention of working together for the good of our families and neighbours in Lydd. I believed Daniel had become my friend, but he is a man who sneaks about making trouble for others. There is no good reason for his actions. No good reason at all.

I have jumped ahead and first I must return to what happened yesterday.

It had seemed like a good day. We made great progress on the two plots of land, each one of them being worked until dusk. With Daniel gone to Lydd, Edwin came to labour in his place and Friar Matthew, who often has a reason to be elsewhere, remained with us. By the time we had finished for the day and walked to the creek to wash, we had cleared three quarters of those first two plots.

"At this rate we may be starting on the third by tomorrow afternoon," John had said.

I felt jubilant.

As well as going to Lydd for supplies, Daniel had been fishing. For supper we enjoyed fish and flatbreads, while the talk revolved around who he had seen, and the messages passed about.

"I didn't see your father, of course," Daniel stated. "But Joan of Langport came to the beach. She asked after you and told me Martin has been in good spirits. He is forced to remain in his bed or in a chair with his leg elevated but tells her what needs doing, and she thinks that she does enough to please him."

"What did you tell Joan about me?"

"I told her about our home here in the copse, that the soil is rich and not too sticky, and how hard you work alongside the men clearing the land."

I considered this, and after a moment Daniel continued, "I said nothing else."

"I'm sure father was glad to have news of me," I replied. What did he mean by those last words? Did he refer to our earlier conversation about Jeb? I felt certain that Daniel wanted me to ask for his reassurance that my father had not been told about Jeb, but I would not do that.

Everyone wanted to speak to Daniel that evening. He commanded the conversation around the fire, and that was no bad thing. There were messages for everyone and for the first time in days we spoke of our lives away from here, rather than concentrating on our tasks and hopes for Middle Isle.

Jeb was quiet, and I wondered if he felt sad to think of us all having friends and family across the water, whereas in Romney there was no one who cared about him. He stayed with us to eat, and then we all walked to the wooden cross and gave our thanks for the food we had received from Lydd, the fish caught by Daniel and the plots of land almost ready for the plough. Afterwards, Jeb slipped away to his fireside and cosy shelter.

Today, as we wiped our plates clean with bread and rested for a short time in the middle of the day, a small boat landed on our beach. We hadn't thought to keep a lookout on our land, being a peaceful group, not warriors. No one knew Amory of Langport had stepped into the shallows and was making his way up the slight rise towards our camp.

"Good day!"

We all rose in unison and John stepped forward, with Edwin and Luke not far behind. I looked around those remaining at the fireside and noted the uncertainty on Jeb's face. Then I realised that Daniel had not joined the other men and I wondered if he had known Amory had planned to visit, and if so, why he had not mentioned it. Glancing from Daniel to Jeb, I felt a chill running through my body.

"I had to come to see this land for myself!" Amory continued. The men responded eagerly, and I listened carefully, trying to work out Amory's true reason for being here. They spoke only of our sheltered area under the trees and the progress we were making in the fields.

I relaxed and started to help Eve gather the plates. Jeb went to draw water from the well, and I was glad that he found something to occupy himself.

"We must return to work," John said after a short time. "But let me show you the far end of the island where Friar Matthew now has a cross and an altar stone, then the creek where we wash, before I join the others."

They left, speaking amicably, John pointing in the direction of the sandy rise where Friar Matthew makes his devotions.

Back working on the land, I could not help but feel resentful that our progress was slowed by John not being with us.

"I didn't expect anyone to come over yet," Luke said, referring to Amory being on the Isle.

I didn't reply. He must have noticed how my shoulders slumped a little and I no longer lifted and carried each clod with ease. My spirits were low as I reflected on what brought Amory of Langport to Middle Isle. Gazing towards Jeb, I saw that his smile which usually came so readily had vanished. I wanted to say something to him, to reassure him that he was welcome here. But how could I when I could not settle my own feelings of unease?

When they reappeared, John and Amory strode along side-by-side, John pointing out the plots. He gestured as if explaining how we started at one end and worked towards the other. I wondered if they deliberated what to do with the mound of grass, tenacious roots and earth, steadily growing as we cleared the land.

We paused in our cutting, digging and carrying. I glanced at my fellow workers. Edwin and Luke appeared relaxed, but there was a twist to Daniel's mouth as if trying to contain a smirk. He was waiting for, or expecting, a reaction to Jeb being here. Amory of Langport had chosen each man and woman who came to Middle Isle. He had not chosen Jebediah.

On the open land, Jeb had nowhere to hide. Nor could he busy himself with any other task than the moving of clods. Everyone else had stopped in their labours and so he waited, his attention seeming to focus on scraping earth from his shoes, but, no doubt, alert to every movement and every word from Amory.

"People of Middle Isle, I am impressed!" Amory stated on reaching the edge of the first plot. "This is good soil, and we did right in coming here. There is one of you who I do not know but has become a friend to everyone here and works as hard as the rest of you. Jebediah of Romney, we are lucky to have you, and glad of all the effort you are putting into our venture. In Lydd, we are so used to soil which is loose with stones and sand, that we know little of a land with heavy earth. How our goats would love this grass! But for you who need to clear it, the work is arduous, and we are blessed to find Jebediah here as our friend not our enemy." Amory skirted the plot and stood as close to Jeb as he could without muddying his shoes more than necessary. "I know John is anxious to get back to work. Jebediah, would you walk back to my boat with me and tell me about yourself?"

"I'd be glad to," Jeb replied, his voice gruff as if he found the words stuck in his throat. He wiped his hands on a patch of grass and joined Amory.

"Good health to you all!" Amory of Langport called out, then he and Jeb turned and made their way back to the beach.

A feeling of heaviness pressed upon my limbs. Amory had not come to make trouble for us. The trouble was already here.

No sooner had we turned back to our work than John strode up to Daniel. I know John as a passive man, but now he stood within an arm's length and bellowed. "What did you hope would come of this? Did you want a good man, a decent man who has done you no harm, to be forced to leave? Or to live alongside us but without the companionship we can offer? Without new people coming into our lives or us going to their towns and villages, how will we ever learn about the world?"

"I didn't tell Amory to come here." Daniel stepped back.

"But you went to him, didn't you? You went to him and told him there was someone else here. What else did you say?"

"I don't trust Jeb."

"I've been appointed the leader here. If you have a concern, then you speak to me."

"What would Martin say?"

"Martin would be pleased to see how we are progressing and that we have a willing helper."

"But what would he..." Daniel looked towards me and stopped. "I understand now. Jeb is welcome here. I thought Amory would want to know." He took the spade and started jabbing at the ground, cutting a square and levering it for Edwin to move, then starting on the next.

John shrugged, gathered a lump of earth and grass in his hands, then moved away. We worked in silence. Luke and I on one plot, John, Daniel and Edwin on the other. Friar Matthew joined us, and Edwin left – our need for a permanent shelter was pressing.

As I worked, I glanced at Luke and wondered if, as Daniel's cousin, he shared a dislike for Jeb. Over the next few days, would we find ourselves a divided settlement, with each one of us choosing who to side with?

# Meg

Another week has gone by, which makes it our third week and before long a cycle of the moon will have passed. Once more Daniel has returned to Lydd for supplies. This time Eve went with him leaving Sarah, who often works on the land with us, in charge of our midday meal.

The first week I stayed on Middle Isle believing that as a family of settlers we would always live and work in harmony. Now I understand we will have our difficulties, and some might work harder than others to keep the peace. John is a good man, with a steady temperament, but he is not a natural leader, having slipped into that role when my father was unable to be here. There is an uneasy truce between Daniel and Jeb, but I have noticed that Jeb is careful to sit away from Daniel when we all relax at the fireside.

I find myself liking Luke more and more. Every day he greets Jeb with a wide smile, often walking to meet him, so Jeb joins us in our camp with a friend beside him. In doing this, Luke faces the quiet fury of his cousin, but has seen there is nothing to dislike about Jeb and no reason not to trust him. Luke is young: sixteen years, I think. I would have expected him to side with his cousin, to be sharing secretive talks and fuelling the fire of Daniel's dislike for Jeb, but he hasn't. Without his support, Daniel is on his own with his prejudices.

We three – Jeb, Luke and I – have finished clearing the first plot and have started the awkward task of ploughing it. With the men taking it in turn to be the human ox, and the other guiding the blade, we trail back and forth, at first leaving thin, uneven lines on the earth and then adding more weight to the back and pressing deeper. Behind them, I work with a rake, breaking down the clods, and appreciating the richness of the soil. As we toil, the men joke and laugh, while we keep an eye on the second plot and a friendly rivalry grows.

Luke and I found our friendship with Jeb rewarded when today he invited us to see his home on the sandy tip of our isle.

"Come and see my home... my place..." Jeb suggested as he strode away from the patch of ploughed land. "After we've eaten maybe."

I wondered if he chose to invite us on this day when Daniel was absent.

"I'd like that. Thank you," I said.

"I might come and live with you," Luke suggested. "I don't know how a man is meant to sleep with John and Friar Matthew snoring all night. I give John a push sometimes, but the monk is too far away."

"You'll see there's only room for one," Jeb was quick to tell him.

We ate with enjoyment. Afterwards I noticed Jeb speaking with John, and then he gestured for Luke and me to join him. We left the copse and walked towards the altar stone and cross where Friar Matthew kneels to pray. From this highest point on the island, we continued just a few steps until the land dropped away.

I frowned. "I can't see your home!"

"I know!" Jeb grinned.

I realised that we were following a track, the grass worn and yellow sand exposed. It sloped downwards, taking us through a patch of scrubby bushes and, when we paused, I looked back to see the monk and his holy place were hidden by those low bushes. The land flattened before sloping once more, this time towards the beach. Once on this shelf of grass and sand, we turned back again and saw a flap of ripped sail hanging down from a piece of curved wood which I knew had come from that boat found on the beach.

"It's dug into the sand!" Luke exclaimed.

"I told you it was!" Jeb retorted.

"You found a sail too," I said, marvelling at his luck. "It makes a good door."

"Take a look." Jeb lifted the sail, throwing it back and across the top of his home, and we crowded either side of him, peering into the cavern.

The bed, running the width of the hollow, looked to be snug. Like us, Jeb had made a mattress of dead leaves, and while this lay thick on the ground, he had just one blanket. I wanted to ask how he managed to stay warm at night, but knew he had no choice other than to bear the cold. He had what he had carried with him or found washed up on the tide, and nothing else.

A pole ran the shallow depth of the place and on it the salvaged fleece hung low over the end of the bed. "You were lucky to find this," I commented.

"I came here with almost nothing, so this is a great prize!" Jeb reached out to touch the wool. "It took a long time to fully dry."

"What's all this?" Luke asked.

In the narrow space between us and the bed, there stood a crate and in it an assortment of objects – from tools crafted by Jeb during his time here to pieces of wood, metal and material that he had found.

"Things I've collected. Some of them seem to hold no use for me, but perhaps they will one day..."

Luke and I had intruded on his sanctuary long enough and we moved outside, skirting the fire pit. I would have loved us to sit on the sandy bank and gaze across the river to the new town of Romney. We could have spoken without fear of Daniel's disapproval and learnt more about Jeb's time here before we arrived. But suddenly I felt uncomfortable about us scrutinising Jeb's home and aware of the work still to be done on the land.

"We must go," I said. "Back to the plots." My words sounded awkward. Rushed.

"Meg only thinks of our land and the crops which will grow!" Luke said, his voice merry. "But she is right."

"No, she thinks of other things," Jeb insisted. "But John is a good man, and it is not fair that we rest while he works."

"Perhaps I do think of the land too much," I responded as we scrambled up the bank. "My father is back there," I gestured towards Lydd, "and he's relying on me."

"I hope you receive good news from him," Jeb said, his tone serious now. "To break a leg is a terrible thing when a man needs to work and provide for his family."

"I hope so too. But he faces several weeks of rest." I pictured Father sitting on the bed, his leg held in place by a frame, only moving when necessary.

Now we near the time when seeds will be planted in both plots, and it is my responsibility to choose wisely. In another week, the third plot will have been prepared. Although the weather has been mild, I must not be hasty and rush my planting. Only the hardiest can be sown. A frost could kill a row of tender seedlings and my fellow settlers would begin to doubt my skills.

"Next time Daniel goes to Lydd, I'll go with him," I declared. "By then some of the bulbs and seeds will have been planted. Father will want to hear about it."

# Meg

I have a patch of worked land, just one yard in width and five long. It lies not far from the thorn bushes, in a slight hollow, and catches the sun from the south while being protected from the wind. As I crumble soil into the finest dust, I can watch the men work. They are digging the third plot, and the monk is scattering lengths of seaweed onto freshly turned soil. Sometimes it glistens in the sun, and I picture the glossy brown pods, some lying in curls and others stretched out. Friar Matthew has provided me with thinner strands for my sheltered seedbed, and amongst the brown there are bright green, feathery lengths. Over the weeks and months ahead, the soil will consume the seaweed and be all the richer for it.

Another week has passed and tomorrow I'll go to see my father. I feel uneasy though. It will be just Daniel and me on his boat. When I should be looking forward to seeing Father, my thoughts keep returning to the time I'll be alone with Daniel.

I stray.

It's relaxing here on my own with the sun warming my skin. We mostly work in our shifts, discarding outer layers as the earth is never kind to our clothes. With the days becoming longer, Sarah has started bringing ale to quench our thirst midway through the morning and afternoon. The third plot is almost clear and would have been finished if we had not suffered three days of torrential rain. However, our time was not wasted, and everyone worked with Edwin until the frame of our longhouse was completed. The roof has its main beams, but there are more to come. Edwin is currently using branches as extra support. He says it doesn't matter if they twist a little, the wood is strong and as long we have something to attach the thatch to then it will suit us well. In the copse there was one huge fallen tree. Edwin had already started making clever use of it by cutting planks and we were able to enclose both ends of the house. The front and rear will be clad over the coming weeks, although not entirely, as the central area will remain open. When we sit around the fire in its new position, we will look out and across the river towards the old port of Romney.

Where the creek cuts into our land, and in other areas around the Isle, reeds have grown thick. Last year's are ready to be cut and tightly bound as thatch. Sarah and Friar Matthew are harvesting them, when they are not busy with their other tasks, and stacking bundles ready to be lashed to the roof timbers.

From my patch where I dig and rake the soil, I can't see the longhouse, but I can hear Edwin working on it. There is usually someone else with him and I hear them call to one another. The scrape of his saw cutting into the wood, or the short bursts of his hammer, mingle with the sounds of domestic life within the copse – the clank of the bucket lowered into the well, the chopping of vegetables on a slab of wood, and Eve talking as she works tirelessly to keep us all fed. These sounds fill the air, creating a comforting backdrop and a reminder of how far we have come in creating our community. Sarah passes by regularly and our friendship grows as we exchange the latest news of the land and our camp, occasionally sharing our private thoughts.

Often our conversations are not completed in the short time Sarah lingers, but opinions are aired and expanded on throughout the day. She ponders on our new shelter of planks and thatch which will, at first, be divided using our woollen sheeting as curtains to pull across the two sleeping areas.

"It will be the same as it is now in the tents," Sarah mentioned, unnecessarily, while on her way to the creek. "Women in one part and men in the other."

"You want to be with Edwin," I stated. I wish she were with her husband because to have him shuffling into our tent at night disturbs both my sleep and my thoughts.

"It won't happen!" She looked towards the camp and lowered her voice. "It's not right, is it? The monk sharing with the other men. They are not monks. It will be him next – he'll have his own shelter."

"That's what John says." I considered the two sleeping spaces and their use. "Perhaps they can be divided into four, two for you who are married, one for the men and one for me." I would be on my own, but not lonely as the others would be close.

"Perhaps," Sarah echoed. Then picking up her bucket of dirty stockings and shifts, she continued to the creek.

Sometime later, when the clothes had been pummelled by hand on the smooth stones by the water's edge, and the water partly wrung out, Sarah returned. This time her bucket was cumbersome, the material still heavy with water, and she was glad to stop.

"They won't allow it," she proclaimed.

"Allow it?" I repeated, easing myself up so I stood, then leaning down to rub my calves.

"For you to be on your own."

"I'd be safe."

"I think John would want to speak with your father... and Amory, if you were thinking of marrying..."

I frowned, unable to make any sense of her words. "Marrying?" All thoughts of planting the leek seeds and wondering if the soil was warm enough vanished. "Why would I?"

"Not yet," Sarah continued, "but you and Jeb? You like him. Everyone likes him, apart from... but that doesn't matter. I don't know what Amory would say for two reasons – we are here to work, and we don't know where he comes from. Romney, of course, but where else?"

I felt a warm flush rise through my neck and to my face. Words began to form in my mind but remained unvoiced. I hadn't thought of marriage, only that I admired him. It didn't mean that... Nothing had been said. I didn't know if he...

"Then there's Daniel. He's watching and he doesn't like it."

"Daniel!" I spluttered. "No! I thought we could be friends here, but he can't be trusted. He showed that when he spoke out about Jeb being here."

"He wants you, Meg. Just be careful. Be careful he doesn't trick you into anything."

I placed my hands on my burning cheeks, trying to cool them. "It's all so difficult," I admitted. "Of course I like Jeb. We work together, him, Luke and I, and we have become friends. But I'm rarely alone with him."

"Island life doesn't allow for it," Sarah admitted. "It doesn't allow for a husband and wife to spend time alone either. We work, we eat, we work, we sleep, and on a Sunday... well, there's still so much to be done. But that's the day to be alone with Jeb. On the day when Daniel still fishes and we can rest a little."

She was right. There is little privacy for those who want or need it here on Middle Isle. Only Jeb has his own place to retreat to. He is here with us but not truly part of our group... our family.

I didn't reply, merely murmured my agreement. Sarah didn't have time to dissect my possible romance and the person who might want to destroy it. She had clothes to spread out to dry and would then move on to the next task. "Will you help me carry this back?" she asked. "It's too heavy."

For now, the confusing talk of myself and Daniel and Jeb ended. I needed time to think carefully on my own. After many years of living with my father, I was unused to idle talk. We never spoke of romance, only the practical side of getting married. 'We must think about you marrying a sensible man,' Father would say on occasion. 'Steer clear of the Woodmans and young Richard. He is too foolish.' If not Richard the Younger, then similar comments about some other man would be expressed, until I was left feeling that no one would ever meet with my father's approval.

One of the problems with living in Lydd is that newcomers rarely come to the town. It is so isolated from the rest of Kent, almost surrounded by the grey sea which beats against the shingle banks at Dengemarsh, and the sluggish River Rother on the other.

When we settled on Middle Isle, I only thought of the land and the plans Father and I had made.

I hadn't considered that anyone else would already be on the Isle.

I hadn't known about Jeb. Or Daniel's hostile nature towards newcomers and his possessive interest in me.

This is all too confusing. This afternoon I shall plant dark, gnarled leek seeds, and tomorrow I shall be on the boat to Lydd, eager to tell Father all about our farming here. That is what is important to me.

# Martin

After three long weeks, my daughter has been to see me. I didn't know if she would – there is so much to do on the island and her skills are needed there.

In the short time we had there was so much to talk about. Meg told me how rich the soil is and how it clings to the roots of the grass and weeds, how heavy the clods are to lift and how sticky it became after the heavy rains. She has planted onion bulbs, turnip and parsnip seeds. Within a day or so, it will be the turn of the carrots and peas. I forgot the cabbage! The cabbage seeds have been sown too. In a month, root vegetable seeds and peas will be planted once more, extending the harvest.

There is no doubt that the crops will flourish, and Daniel will be bringing food to us in Lydd rather than collecting it for those living on Middle Isle.

Meg explained everything, her words tumbling out, showing her passion for the land. For a while I forgot the nagging pain in my leg and the frustration I feel at having to depend on Joan of Langport for everything. That woman is a saint to put up with my bad temper. She brings me remedies to aid the healing and ensures that I am as comfortable as possible. We talk about our lives and wonder about those on Middle Isle or, to break the monotony, play games with dice and counters. What a fool I was to climb on the roof and an even bigger fool to slip off, but I have been blessed by having Joan here with me.

Meg left as quickly as she arrived, and Joan returned shortly after, having collected the eggs and milked the goats.

"How was Meg?" she asked, her eyes bright and voice eager. "I didn't want to interrupt."

"There are three plots cleared and ploughed," I told her. "Three plots of half an acre each. It's not like here where the soil barely grips the roots. It's good soil, firm and rich, although that does mean more work for them all as they clear it. They've sown onion bulbs, turnip and parsnip seeds. And there's a small plot in a hollow where she has put the leek seeds."

"We can imagine it now," Joan replied. "Surely, they haven't planted all the plots? Not yet."

"Not yet," I agreed. "The first two are for vegetables, and there is more to do. The third will be for barley, which must be sown soon and in deep drills. Meg knows that. Once it is harvested in the late summer, they can set about making ale."

"Is half an acre enough?"

"I doubt it. Not when they need it for their broth too. They hope to prepare another plot, but it may not be in time for the spring sowing."

"And more for winter barley?"

"Aye! How wonderful it was to see Meg. Those other messages... they weren't the same, were they? Better to see her."

"You've told me all about the land," Joan responded, "but how is Meg in herself? Does she like it there, living with the others? Is she happy?"

I considered her words and frowned, at first not quite understanding – if the land is good then Meg should be happy. After all, that is the reason for her being there.

"I think so," I replied. "It is all going as we planned."

"That's good." Joan leaned over, taking some of my weight as she helped me ease myself into a different position on the bed. "I hope they're all content across the water." She nodded towards the Isle.

"I didn't have time to ask about everything," I admitted, while tucking the blanket around myself. "But I have a feeling there is something Meg didn't tell me."

# Meg

What could I do? If I wanted to see my father, I had no choice but to travel with Daniel. I felt uncomfortable from the start, but never expected him to start talking about our future.

Our future – me and him.

Why would he think...? We've never been friends... I liked him better when we began making plans for me to go to Middle Isle, but he soon spoilt that. Now he has made it worse than before we came here.

I didn't tell Father, of course. Hopefully I can persuade Daniel to stop this foolish talk. But perhaps I should have said something, should have warned Father, just in case Daniel went to him as he had suggested he would.

Daniel won't. Not now. Will he?

# Daniel

I thought it best to talk to Meg when we were alone in the boat. I know there are only eight of us on the island, nine when *he* is with us, but we don't get any time alone. Luke and Meg work with *him* on the first plot and John is with the monk on the second plot. Yesterday, I assumed I could speak to her when she was on her own attending to the seed bed, but Sarah kept passing by.

It didn't go well, this talk on the boat. I thought she had more sense, but living out there by the Rype with Martin has given Meg more spirit than I like in a woman. If she lived in the town amongst other women or had a mother to guide her, then she would have responded differently – she would have wanted to please me.

"How many years are you?" I asked not long after we left the beach.

"Twenty-one," she replied.

"You haven't married."

"I haven't."

I heaved on the oars, lifted them and guided them into the water again, then repeated the process.

"You've had to look after your father, of course."

She seemed to ponder on this for a moment. "Aye. There's so much to do and just us to do it. Thankfully Joan is there now. I wonder how she is managing… how he is managing…"

"He's a freeman. You have a good amount of land," I said, wanting to keep to the point. "I have this boat and we do well with the fishing and smoking but it's a different life. Anyway, that's all changed. Now we are on Middle Isle, and everyone is the same. There are no freemen or barons. We are all working together."

"There's Friar Matthew," she said. "He's different and will have his own place to sleep soon, away from the rest of the men."

"True," I replied. "It's not right though… not right how it is. Man and wife should be together. There will be more changes over time."

"The land must come first," she responded without hesitation.

"We're all the same now," I repeated. "No one better. No one owning more land than the other on the island. I'd like to speak to your father about this – to explain how it is."

"Why?" she asked.

"Because there's no reason why you and I can't marry. We have witnesses on the island, and I have a ring to gift you. It's here with me now. I'm a hard worker, Meg, and don't forget I spoke to Amory about you coming along with us. I did it because I like you. So, I'll speak to Martin when I return to Lydd next week."

"Marry?" she said, her voice unmistakably flat. "I don't know that I want to marry. It's not fair to say it just like that. There's no need to speak to Father. He wants to know about the land, not these plans of yours that I have not agreed to."

She needs time to think about it. I'll speak to Martin next time, but before that I'll speak to John and Edwin about the longhouse. It should be divided differently. Meg and I will need our own bed when we're married.

# Meg

"Go to Jeb. Go while Daniel is away fishing," Sarah whispered to me as we strolled away from the wooden cross having thanked the Lord for the mild weather, the good soil, and prayed for the success of those first seedlings. Almost a week had passed since I visited my father, and we were becoming more settled in our roles on the Isle.

"What reason do I have?" My heart began to quicken.

"The wool! He has a fleece. Offer to help him comb it... or pull it into yarn."

"But I am needed..."

"You are not needed. This is our time to rest."

I allowed myself no time to think. Jeb had already separated himself from the rest of our group. On other days he worked alongside us, his place in our family accepted. But on a Sunday I sensed he became unsure of his role and retreated to his own place. I changed direction and fell into step beside him.

"You do so much to help us, I wondered... is there anything... would you like me to help with the fleece you told me about?"

"The fleece?" A smile spread across Jeb's face. "I hardly know how to make a start. I've washed it and picked out most of the dirt."

"Then it needs combing."

"I've started making a comb... or two... I'll need two. John has given me some long nails and I've hammered a few through a piece of wood." He paused, and I imagined he was considering his progress so far. "There is no handle, and the nails may work lose."

Now out of sight from the others, we were walking down the sandy slope towards his secluded shelter. I considered the makeshift comb. "If the wood is young then hopefully it will grip for a while."

"I think you're right," Jeb agreed. We neared his home, and he indicated the shelf or bench shaped in the sandy bank. "Would you like to sit here?" he asked. "It's quite dry and makes a pleasant place to rest."

Nudging aside the curtain to his shelter, Jeb entered the cave-like place and the curtain fell back. Almost immediately he was pushing his way out again, this time with the huge fleece in his arms. "I don't have a bag for it, and during the coldest nights

I spread it out to use as a blanket. But if it could be made into a cloak, that would be a fine thing!"

I stood and reached out, burrowing my fingers into the wool, tugging it apart. The oil within it immediately spread to my dry hands. "I would love to work with this," I told him. "I agree, a cloak would be fine, but look here..." I showed him the undercoat, an area of denser but finer wool. "If we were to separate this, then we could make a new shift as well."

"We?" he asked, smiling at me across the bulk of the fleece.

"As the evenings become longer, I would gladly help you." I pictured us sitting in companionable silence while we first worked the wool into a yarn and later wove a cloth for a cloak, then a shift. Perhaps, when the summer sun parched the land, we would move to other parts of the island, to take in different views and to catch the best of the light. The sunsets were glorious, but Jeb's sandy bench faced towards the east.

"I don't expect you to..." Jeb began.

"But I'd enjoy it!" I insisted. "You won't be dyeing the yarn, will you?"

"There is no need."

"Then it has been washed enough, and when I work on it the oil will soothe my dry skin. That's why

I would be glad to do it." I stepped back, my fingers sliding out of the wiry wool.

"Thank you." His response was brief, but his smile and the warmth in his eyes hinted that he was not only grateful for my help but looked forward to the time we would spend together.

"Next time Daniel goes to Lydd, Eve will go with him," I said. "I'll ask her to bring metal combs. It will make working the wool much easier."

"Should we wait?" he looked disappointed.

"Proper combs will be easier to use, but first we must separate this dense undercoat, and that can be done with our hands. Let's use this time we have today."

Perching on the seat, with the fleece between us, Jeb and I faced the estuary. Nearby, the tide flowed high, rippling in the shallows as it reached the dark golden sands. Boats bobbed about in the direction of the river mouth and a couple sailed inland, but they kept to the deeper channel near Romney, and no one aboard could have spotted us on what appeared to be a lonely island. The breeze brought with it the salty scent of the sea and no longer carried the vicious nip of an icy chill. Gulls swooped, and a family of sandpipers scurried on the beach.

While working the fleece, pulling apart the undercoat with its finer, crinkly hair, we spoke first of mundane things – the anticipated seedlings which would show themselves any day now, the lack of thatch for the roof of our shelter taking shape in the camp, the success of the well – and then about ourselves and our lives before we met here on Middle Isle.

Back in the copse, Sarah was preparing dinner with help from Luke. A few weeks earlier, John had declared that we three women should not have to labour over the cooking pot on the day of rest. "You are all working hard and should take your turn to rest on the sabbath. Daniel fishes on a Sunday, so there are eight of us left now Jebediah is with us. Two of us will prepare the midday meal and supper, leaving the others free to do as they wish."

With the undercoat and main body of wool separated, and the stories of our lives barely touched upon, there came the clatter of a stick on a metal pan.

"Food!" Jeb stood, gathering the main bulk in his arms. "We must go. I wonder... would you have time... afterwards?"

"We could start the combing," I suggested. "I'm not sure if the nails will hold, but we can try."

We bundled the fleece back into the shelter and scrambled up the bank, our backs now turned to the coast. As we passed the wooden cross on the stone altar, we didn't notice a small sailing boat riding high on the tide having left the old port of Romney not long before.

# Henry of Romney

My daughter, Judith, has travelled from Hythe with her husband, arriving at my home not long after I broke my fast this morning. They stayed overnight in the new port of Romney and plan to return there tonight. It has been many years since I last saw her. So many that I have often wondered if she were still alive. So many that I wondered if those lies I told her son had become the truth. I thought it best if he believed her to be gone.

She brought with her one child – just the one after all these years – a girl of five years.

"Have you seen him? Has Jebediah been here?" Judith asked before any news had been exchanged and her daughter had been introduced.

"I've not seen him." I shrugged my shoulders. "Perhaps he chooses to live with his own kind?"

"His own kind?" she spat back at me. "I am his mother and you, his grandfather. We are his kind. I thought you would have told him I had gone to Hythe. Told him that my husband will welcome him in our home, as we said he would. Every day I pray that Jebediah will come to me and, although I have been too sick... too frail to travel to Romney, that he would come to see his mother. But I have not seen him. Has he not been here at all?"

"I have not seen him." The lie came easily.

I offered them wine, and she calmed down a little. I learnt the child is called Isabel, but she was too shy to speak to me and remained hiding within the folds of Judith's cloak. My son by marriage and I discussed business matters, he being a cloth merchant, and together they spoke about their home town, and their home near the strand.

As time passed and the broth prepared by a local woman simmered over the fire, I began to relax, believing that Judith's outburst over her firstborn had passed. She had offered to ladle our meal into the bowls and was about to hand Isabel to her father when there came a vicious turn of events.

Even as I tell my story I can barely believe that it could be true. That of all the days... all the moments... it had to be at this time.

A young man, tall and lean with a tangle of hair and an air of importance, rapped on the open door of my home. Before I could respond, he said, "I'm looking for Jebediah of Romney's grandfather. Is this the right place?"

Judith gasped.

"It will be nothing," I told her, walking to the door. "Serve our meal, and I'll speak to this fellow outside."

"Serve the meal?" she repeated. "How many years have I waited for news of my son, and now you expect me to ladle broth?"

Now the stranger stared at Judith, disbelief on his face. "But he said his mother was dead!" He ran a hand through his hair and continued, "Forgive me. I didn't mean to voice my thoughts. I was looking for his grandfather, thinking he was the only relative nearby."

"I am his grandfather," I said. "Who are you?"

Now the three of us stood at the open doorway, with Judith's husband standing behind her and the little girl... well, she cowered somewhere like the timid creature she is.

"Daniel by Rother, fisherman from Lydd," he introduced himself. "I say from Lydd, but we are living on Middle Isle, a group of us. It's just me there with the boat, so I came to say... I thought you would want to know that your grandson... your son... is there. There on Middle Isle!"

"On Middle Isle?" Judith repeated, her voice high. "He has been on Middle Isle these past years... how many have passed? Ten or more."

Now it was Daniel's time to look confused. "Ten years? Nay, he came from here just a few months ago. At least that's what he said. Ten years? It cannot be."

"And where was he before?" Judith asked Daniel.

"Here in Romney, I believe."

What could I do? I was only thinking of my daughter when I said Jebediah had not been here. I was thinking of her marriage to this man of wealth, and how he might reject her if he met Jebediah. "He was here," I began. "But ill. Very ill. I didn't want to upset you. When he left, I assumed he had... that his soul had gone. Gone from this earth." I placed my hand on my chest and gazed upwards.

"My son was here recently?"

Judith has changed. Where she was once a meek little thing, wary of everyone and everything, she has found confidence.

"If we had known of him being here, we would have come before," her husband said, showing his support of her and her first child, now a man, born long before their marriage.

"It was just a short time. A matter of days." I attempted to justify my hiding the news. "Then he was gone." I paused, considering my next words. "Jebediah, your son, was very ill with a fever and prone to wandering. I could not contain him. My manservant fed him, and we sent for tonics, but the last time he was seen... the last place he was seen

148

was on the riverbank at high tide." I stopped, allowing them to imagine the scene.

"He entered the water, and no one tried to stop him?" Judith's husband asked. I have not named him before, as he has a small part in this story, but he is called Alfred, Alfred by Haven.

"No one saw him in the water," I countered. "It was assumed... Later."

"When he didn't return," Judith stated. Then she addressed the fisherman, "Can you take me to him?"

Up to that moment, I hadn't considered the fisherman's place in this tale, only that I would have preferred him not to be a witness to all of this. Now a sense of him not being here to reunite a family, but to make trouble, came to me. Things had gone badly wrong for Daniel as they had for me. But what was his motivation in coming to Romney? He must have wanted Jebediah gone from Middle Isle, or to learn something that would put my grandson at a disadvantage in that place where he had settled. Instead, he met a mother eager to see her son and a wealthy merchant from Hythe, here in support of his wife.

"Take you?" Daniel repeated. This meeting was not going as he planned. "I must leave now, while the tide is high, and the boat has fish in it... Perhaps tomorrow?"

"I live by the sea and am not concerned about fish," Judith declared.

What have the folk of Hythe done to my daughter who left here so shy and pliable?

"The tide is falling fast," Alfred by Haven said. "If you go, you will not be able to return today. Is there somewhere she can stay? I have never heard of this Middle Isle. Does it have shelter and beds for visitors?"

"Nay, it is just the eight of us living in tents for the past few weeks," Daniel explained. "Eight of us from Lydd and Jeb, but he is in his own place – no more than a hollow. You are right about the tide, and I must go." He began to edge away.

"Then I will find a man to take us there tomorrow," Alfred said.

"Tomorrow?" Judith echoed, her tone anxious.

"Tomorrow. It is but one day and you have waited years to see your son."

Now, some hours later, my daughter has returned to the new town of Romney with her husband and the child, who I think they said was called Isabel. I stand by the glistening mudflats, gazing past the deep channel of water, then across the shallows to Middle Isle. Is there a ribbon of smoke rising from the island? Or do I just imagine it?

I cannot think that any good can come of Judith and Jebediah meeting after all this time. At least no good to me. Alfred says they will pay a man from downriver, at the new port of Romney, to take them to Middle Isle. I see no way of preventing this and no way of persuading Judith that I think only of her good.

# Meg

We have been blessed with mild weather since being on Middle Isle. When it rains, we are showered for a short time and then the sun returns. My seeds and onion bulbs must be thriving in the rich soil, and I can't wait to see green shoots emerge. All morning, John, Luke, Jeb and I have been pressing a stick deep into the earth of the third plot, planting barley seeds and repeating the process. Every so often one of us rakes over the land.

Meanwhile, Edwin continues to make our wooden home with help from Friar Matthew and Daniel, although Daniel has now left to go fishing.

As I work, I find my thoughts roaming from one man to the other. Mostly I think of Jeb and how much I enjoyed spending time with him yesterday. When we have combs for the fleece, it would do no harm for us to work on it for a short time in the evening before sunset. There is no need for a good light. I catch his eye as we work on the land, and we exchange smiles as if we have a shared secret. There is no secret, only that I am thinking of being alone with him again.

Sometimes I think of Daniel and find myself disturbed by him. It has been three days since he spoke of marriage to me. How am I to know if he has put those thoughts aside or if he has spoken to John and still plans to talk to my father? Will I find that it has all been agreed before anything else is said to me?

Perhaps I should speak to Eve. Aye, that would be for the best. Then she can tell John that I do not want to marry Daniel.

When he sets off in his boat, part of me is glad that Daniel has left the island, but this comes with the nagging thoughts that he is free to go to Lydd. And once there, what trouble might he spread?

Did Daniel go somewhere yesterday? I thought I knew him well enough, but when he returned with his catch there was something odd... at least not quite right about him. I cannot say what is different, only that he has something on his mind.

# Jebediah

Since the settlers travelled from Lydd, my life on Middle Isle has improved every day. Just one of their eight wants to make trouble for me, but I am blessed with friendship from the others.

I have spent weeks, sometimes months, aboard ships with only boys and men for company. Over time I noticed the women we met at the docks, but there was never time to strike up a friendship. Many of the sailors scoured the alehouses and alleys of every port for a woman who was willing to pleasure them in her bed or some cosy corner of a barn, but not me. I kept to myself, avoiding the taverns and the women. I was used to a life at sea and, as I changed from boy to man, the other sailors respected me, but perhaps I was waiting for a different life. A place on land to make my home.

It has been good these past weeks, but I don't know if these people plan to live on Middle Isle after the first crops have been harvested. They don't seem to know themselves what will happen, and I don't ask. Back in Lydd they have homes and families to return to, and the friar will move on, in his own time, to preach in other towns and villages and spread the word of the places he has seen. It is people like me and him, the travellers, who tell the others about the world.

Meg will return to her father. At least I assume she will. They have their own land, although she says there is better soil on the island. It may be richer here, but they understand the earth they farm and make the most of it. I can't help wondering if there might be a place for me over the water in Lydd, if Martin at Rype would welcome me. Amory of Langport has shown friendship and that will pave my way.

Yesterday, while we worked the fleece, Meg told me about how she used to stand on the shore of the Rother and gaze across to the Isle. Now we stand on Middle Isle and look back to the places we lived before, or sometimes gaze inland to where the hills rise on the edge of this marshy land. I wonder if Meg would like to visit other places – I'll ask her next time we are alone.

This morning, we started early, planting barley seeds under Meg's guidance. After a while, we paused to sup ale and munch on soft apples which came to the island in the last food crate from Lydd. By the time we were back to work, a small fishing boat could be seen gliding along the Rother in the direction of Broomhill.

"He's in a funny mood." Luke nodded towards the boat.

I couldn't see the figure on board but assumed it was Daniel. It wasn't my business to comment, so I said nothing.

But Meg, who had known Daniel all her life, asked, "Has he said anything to you, Luke? I have a feeling there's something on his mind."

"I think you're right," Luke told her. "I reckon he's looking for trouble again, but he's not said anything to me."

Work took Luke away from us as he picked up the rake and began to drag loose soil over the surface until it filled the holes and the seeds lay covered.

"We don't really know, do we?" Meg said to me. "We don't know where he goes once he's sailed off."

Daniel was gone for a while and that was good enough for me, so I changed the subject. "Did you ask Eve about the combs. Then we can work on the fleece again, if you'd like to?"

"I did and I'd like that," she replied. "Just think, by the time it's combed, the seedlings will be showing all over here." She gestured to the other plots. Every day we scanned the bare earth for the sight of the first green shoots.

Whether we work on the land here on Middle Isle, across the water in Lydd, or some other place unknown to us, if it is with Meg, then my life will be blessed. I look forward to our evenings combing the fleece and talking of our lives before we both journeyed to Middle Isle.

# Meg

The most incredible thing happened just before we stopped work at midday. There we were planting seeds and raking the ground, occasionally passing a comment, and frequently pausing to stand straight and rub the small of our aching backs, when a boat landed on the shore.

At first, assuming Daniel was returning, although he had not long left, we paid little attention. But as soon as it grounded on the sand, it was clear the vessel carried more than one person – three in fact. The view from our plots of land to the beach was clear and we watched as two men hauled the boat through the shallows and then a women climbed out.

"What's all this about?" John asked, partly to himself. "I can't say I know them."

We stood with tools and sacks of seed in our mucky hands, all facing the strangers. In turn, they looked in our direction before exchanging a few words. Then one stayed with the boat, while a man and the woman started walking towards us.

"I'll go and see what they want," John said. Once clear of the worked plot of land, his stride lengthened, and we saw him raising his arm in a greeting.

They met midway, on the land where we would one day sow the winter barley. We could hear the woman's voice, anxious as her words poured out, while the man placed a hand on her arm as if to reassure her. John pointed towards the plots where we all stood, the planting forgotten, and they turned. Then the woman broke free of the man's gentle hold and began running towards us. The uneven ground made her approach a little wild as she lurched from tussock to dip. By the time she reached us, her headscarf had fallen to her shoulders revealing thinning mousey hair.

"Jebediah," she called, with desperation in her voice, and we noticed that tears flowed unchecked down her gaunt cheeks.

Luke and I turned to Jeb, who seemed to be confused by the arrival of this woman crying his name with such passion. His mouth opened slightly but no words came, while the frown on his forehead deepened, and his dark eyes stared without blinking. I took a step closer, wanting to reach out to him... to reassure him, yet not knowing if he needed comfort. Then, as the woman spoke again, I noticed that Luke had also moved closer, and now the two of us offered an invisible protection around our friend.

"Jebediah," she repeated. She wiped her cheeks and I noticed that her slender hands were smooth, showing her to be a woman who lived in some comfort. "Do you know me?"

The men were there now, and I glanced at John. His expression showed no concern or unease. In fact, there was a hint of a smile on his rugged face.

"I think so," Jeb replied, his voice gruff as if he had only just found it. "Mother?"

"I didn't know... I thought you would come to me if you could... but you didn't..."

"I thought..." Jeb began, but he stopped, perhaps unable to express his thoughts. Stepping across the divide between them, he placed a hand on her shoulder. "Thank you for coming to find me."

"Let's give them some time alone together," John suggested. "Meg, can you go ahead and tell Eve we have company. Luke and I can finish this row of planting." He turned to the man who I assumed was the husband of Jeb's mother. "Will you stay with us? I'll show you what we are doing here on Middle Isle."

We left the camp this morning to sow barley seeds, and by midday Jeb had learnt his mother is not dead as he believed, but living in Hythe with her husband and young daughter who is being looked after in Romney.

My mind is filled with questioning how this could have happened... how so many years could have passed with both mother and son believing the other to be dead. I wonder if Jeb will now leave Middle Isle and our friendship will end before it has truly begun.

# *John*

I am exhausted. The wonder of Jeb being reunited with his mother did, of course, lead to my questioning how she knew where to find him, and then to the inevitable conclusion that once more Daniel has set out to bring trouble to Middle Isle. No sooner had Jeb left to walk his mother and her husband to the boat than I called a meeting of the settlers.

"I am forced to ask myself how Judith by Haven knew her son was here." I stood under the canopy of a broad oak tree, while the others remained seated around the fire. "It is only us and a few people from Lydd who know about Jebediah. The estuary between Lydd and Romney is wide and news takes its time to travel from one town to the other. Judith and Alfred came from Romney, and it is while they were at the old port that they received the news."

"Do you know how they heard?" Edwin asked.

"A fisherman came and told them," I replied.

"A fisherman went to the old port for that reason?" Luke queried.

"Aye." I paused, hesitant to share my thoughts but knowing they must be aired. "We have a fisherman living here with us who has already been to Lydd and told Amory of Langport about Jeb being here."

"And knowing of the troubles between Jeb and his grandfather, Daniel then sailed to the old port of Romney," Edwin suggested.

"I fear it must be true." I am not a man to state the same thing in different ways. They understood my meaning, and now I awaited their response.

"Daniel is my kin, and it is thanks to him that I am here with you all," Luke began. "But I want to say... I must say... that Jeb is my friend and I... well, I hate the way Daniel has taken against him. I see no reason for it."

"He didn't tell you?" Edwin asked.

"He didn't, and if he had then I would have done my best to stop him."

No one suggested that I was wrong to think badly of Daniel and, having taken a deep breath, I continued. "In my heart, we are all equals here, living together and in peace on this island. But Amory placed me as leader and so I am going to ask you all to consider if you want Daniel to continue living amongst us. If you want him to leave, when he returns with the catch, I will meet him on the beach and return with him to Lydd. I will borrow another boat and come back here tomorrow. So, I ask you now to raise your hand with mine if you want him to be gone."

One by one, the women and Edwin lifted their hands, and I gave a nod in recognition of their support. Friar Matthew shook his head, which I took to mean that he wished to abstain. I looked at Luke and said, "There is no need for you..."

"You must have my answer," he replied. "Daniel is my cousin. But I want to remain here, and you must know that I am loyal to our Middle Isle family and to Jeb." He raised his arm. When he was chosen to join us on the Isle, I wondered if Luke was too young, but he had shown himself to be both a good worker and a friend to us all.

There wasn't much to collect from the tent – some blankets, stockings, a shift and a tunic. Daniel already had his belt at his waist with his knife and wore his thick cloak; most of the fishing tackle was on the boat and was his to take back with him. I considered the poles and netting set up to trap mackerel – poles from our trees here and netting knotted by Eve and Sarah from rope provided by Amory – Daniel could not claim them as his.

They made a crestfallen group – Luke, Meg and the Friar – walking away from the camp, back to the third plot to continue the sowing of the barley. How depleted they were. I trudged past the thorn bushes and across the rough grass to the beach, giving Jeb a brief wave as we passed at a distance.

I didn't have long to wait as one small boat left our shore for Romney, with Jeb's family aboard, and Daniel's boat returned. He must have known that I was wise to his attempt to cause trouble for Jeb, for he kept his gaze averted as the boat neared, the underside scraping on the beach as it came to rest.

The roll of blankets and a sack with Daniel's clothes had been placed on a ribbon of dry shingle. I approached him and, without exchanging any pleasantries, made my feelings clear, "There is no place for you here on Middle Isle. I won't have a traitor in our midst. Your belongings are here. You are to return to Lydd."

He shrugged. "To call me a traitor is unjust. I only want to keep us as one family and for Meg and me to settle here without interference from those who were not meant to be on the island."

His words confused me, and I struggled to grasp his meaning, but then I remembered Eve saying that she was sure Daniel saw his future with Meg, although Meg never gave any encouragement. At the time, when Eve had mentioned it, I had seen no hint of a particular friendship between them, whereas my wife had noticed how Daniel continually watched Meg as she went about her work. Eve had also wondered if there was a growing closeness between

Jeb and Meg, something else that I, with my mind full of cultivating the plots and keeping us warm and dry, had seen nothing of.

"We have spoken of getting married. I plan to give her ring to pledge my commitment," Daniel said before I had time to respond.

With my knowledge of Eve's observations I could reply with confidence, "There will be no vows unless Meg wishes it, and she has had her chance to speak with me about it. Hand over half your catch and take the rest back to Lydd. I think that is fair, don't you?"

Without answering, Daniel hauled his net containing a dozen or so writhing fish over the side, which I retrieved, placing it beyond the high tide mark before returning with his belongings.

"And when I am back in Lydd, do you plan to stay here without a boat?" Daniel asked, clearly sure of his value, or at least that of his boat.

"Nay. I will come with you now, and tomorrow I will return with a boat and another man. It is not your concern."

Now I am in the comfort of my own home, with my forge close by and my sons asking one question after the other. One moment I yearn for my old life, to work with metal rather than dig the land. My temporary forge is set up on the island but has never been used. The next moment, I miss the feeling shared by us all on Middle Isle of new adventures to come. Earlier I went to see Amory, to seek his approval for the choice I have made. He gave it willingly, having met Jeb and liking him for his friendly manner. Tomorrow, at first light, I'll go back to meet Amory and together we will speak with Luke by Rother's family to ask for a boat and another man for our island home.

I will sleep well tonight.

# Meg

Jebediah has not gone. He is still here on Middle Isle. Perhaps he will go, but he did not leave immediately as I feared he might. If Jeb has a new father who is a merchant and can offer him a comfortable home in Hythe, why would he choose to stay here? When I ask myself that question – and I do, over and over – then I hear a little voice in my head. It says: 'He will stay for you.'

We were all uneasy yesterday when John left with Daniel. No one spoke about it, but I think we all grieved for the loss of someone who had been so important to our group. After all, it was Daniel's boat that brought us here and it was he who enabled us to keep our link with Lydd. But, at the same time, it was Daniel's freedom in having the boat which meant he could betray us.

I found myself recalling the time when I decided that I must come here as a replacement for my father. Daniel had gone with me to see Amory, and I thought at the time we would be friends. Did he want me here on Middle Isle because of my knowledge of the land and which crops would thrive, or because he thought there would be no one to object to us living as husband and wife?

Amongst the melancholy there comes great joy. We are pleased for Jeb who has suffered difficulties and lived a lonely life. Now, in the space of weeks, he has gained a new family on the Isle and his true family nearby. We have all talked about Judith's life since she left Romney for Hythe many years ago. What will Jeb's sister think of her brother, and what will he think of her? If he chooses to live in Hythe, what sort of place is it, and will his new father offer him suitable work? Of course, Jeb can answer none of these. He asks himself the very same questions, yet we cannot help wondering.

Yesterday evening, the rain hammered down relentlessly. I prayed that my seeds, their tender shoots and fragile roots were snug within the earth, and no sprouting seeds would be washed away. Jeb had retreated to his sandy hollow, and the rest of us slipped between the folds of our blankets making sure not to touch the tented walls of our shelters.

"We'll be under a thatch roof soon," Eve murmured before drifting off to sleep.

Sarah, who had been binding bundles of reeds more than anyone else, said, "I asked John to bring straw from Lydd... I wonder if he will."

Then they were both asleep, and my thoughts wandered from Jeb to his mother to the wooden walls and thatch roof. Sleep came, but my dreams were vivid and the earth beneath me felt harder than ever. However, the rain eased during the night, and I awoke to clear skies.

Today we all remained within the camp until late morning. Edwin works so hard to make our new home and although he frequently has someone to help him, it is not long before they have to return to their main duties on the land, or some other task which is their main concern. Without complaint, Edwin stays to build our home. Now we are close to its being finished, Eve suggested that if we all work together then one side, or compartment, could be ready for us.

We sometimes call it a longhouse, this shelter we have planned with sleeping areas at either end and a central area which is partly enclosed. Three walls of each sleeping area will be made up of rough wooden planks, and the fourth will be a partition of our woollen tent sheeting. In time, this will be changed to be a solid divide, but for now Edwin must use his skills and our precious wood for other projects.

No one mentioned it, but I think we all worked with extra vigour, wanting to please John on his return. We knew this past day had been difficult for him and imagined his pleasure at seeing the front walls fully clad. As the men cut and shaped planks to fill the last of the gaps, Sarah and I scoured the island for reed stalks which could be bound as thatch. Eve began to clear the women's tent, hauling sacks full of those dry leaves we use as our meagre mattresses.

Friar Mathew walked in his measured pace from the copse to his altar where he prayed for the success of our crops and that our new home would provide us with the shelter needed over the coming months. He returned, working alongside Jeb to strip the woollen sheeting from our tent and hanging it as a curtain across our new sleeping area. I wondered if he thought of having his own private place or cell. Perhaps the strong tent poles would be reused as a frame for this purpose.

"It will be Edwin's next job," Sarah suggested when I mentioned it to her. "A monk wants to be alone or with other monks."

And when Friar Matthew has his own quarters, might Jeb come to live with us? Or might he be gone by then? Thoughts of his plans were never far from my mind.


As the morning progressed, we congratulated ourselves on the changes in our camp and returned to our usual tasks. Eve had a meal to prepare, not just for us but also for Jeb's family who had been invited to join us. This time they were bringing his sister, Isabel, to meet him.

Knowing that the plots offered a clear view of the beach, I suggested that Jeb and I went back to our work on the land. A couple of days before, a fourth half-acre had been marked out and we were keen to start removing the top layer of grass and weeds. The moment he spotted the boat from Romney, Jeb could be waiting on the beach to meet it.

When we left the copse, it was the first time Jeb and I had been alone since his family had arrived the day before.

"You're going to meet your sister soon," I began. "I wonder how she feels."

"It's an odd thing to meet a stranger and be told he's your brother."

"I imagine your mother always spoke of you even if she doubted you would ever meet."

"Do you think so?" Jeb had been looking ahead, but now he slowed his pace and looked at me. "One moment I think my mother is dead, the next she is here. Did she ever try to find me before?"

"If she didn't, then she had good reason not to," I replied. "Your mother came the moment she heard where you were. She thought of you every day you have been apart. I am certain of it."

"Thank you." His response was simple but spoken with emotion.

We walked on, past the thorn bushes, and onto the open land with views across the Rother to Lydd. A small boat could be seen sailing towards us.

"There they are," I said. "By the time we have cleared half a strip, your sister will be here." I walked faster, wanting to make some progress.

Jeb didn't reply. I judged it best to leave him to his own thoughts, and by the time he had loosened the first matted square of grass and weeds, he remarked, "I'm staying here, you know."

"I didn't know," I replied carefully. Avoiding his gaze, I pulled at the clump, tugging at the tangle of roots, and lifted it into my arms.

He plunged the spade into the ground. "I want to be a part of all this." He levered the earth. "With you."

"I'm glad." Turning away, I took a few steps, keeping the grass against my apron. Crumbs of earth scattered to the ground. I dropped it clear of the plot.

"I don't know what is going to happen here," Jeb continued. "The crops will flourish, but will some of you... some of us... stay? You all have homes and family back in Lydd. I think when the autumn comes, there will be decisions to make."

"I didn't expect to stay here. I wasn't even meant to be here," I reminded Jeb. He knew the story of my father's broken leg.

"You'll go back to Lydd." He nudged the next clump towards me with the tip of the spade. "But we have the summer ahead of us before there are choices to be made."

"You would be welcome in Lydd, or with your family in Hythe," I suggested. "Or perhaps you'll stay here. You don't need to decide yet." It was enough to know that he wanted to remain for now and was thinking of a future with me.

By now the sailing boat was close enough to see three figures as well as the boatman. We cut and cleared a few more clumps. Then Jeb wiped his hands on the grass and ran his fingers through his dark, wiry hair. He smiled at me and said, "I'll be off then. But later, if the weather stays fair, perhaps you can help me with the fleece."

"I'd like that."

# Martin

I hear there has been trouble on Middle Isle. The news came to me from Joan, and she heard it from her sister by marriage, Philippa of Langport. Joan is no foolish gossip of a woman and can be trusted to recount exactly what she was told.

Daniel is back in Lydd – that is what she said. Also, there is another man living on the Isle. He has been there all the time our people have been there and longer. I had not known this before, and neither had Joan despite her seeing Amory and Phillipa of Langport several times over the course of the time she has been staying with me.

Now we learn that Amory knew of this man, Jebediah. Amory knew of him and *even* went to meet him on the island. He likes him very much, according to Joan.

John Smithy has stayed overnight in the town and today he is to ask another fisherman to come to Middle Isle with a boat. I suggested to Joan, and she agreed, that Daniel must have done something very wrong to lead to him returning here. As boat-owner his role was essential to the project. At least I believed him to be essential, but most men can be replaced and that is exactly what will happen.

I wonder why Meg didn't mention that there was already someone on the Isle. Was she being secretive about it? Do things happen on Middle Isle that she keeps to herself?

Joan thinks... although she was reluctant to say this at first... she thinks Meg has developed a fondness for Jebediah. I find it strange that Joan should be so sensitive to Meg's feelings. I am a man who only thinks about what he has been told, whereas Joan is conscious of the words which have been left unsaid.

We get along very well, Joan and I. She tolerates my low spirits and understands how I long to be working on my land again. Every fine day, she helps me walk a few steps and settles me on the bench outside my home. Before I am seated, Joan cushions the wood with a folded blanket. If I am to remain in the same position for several hours it is important to be comfortable, she says. In return, I tell her that in all my forty-five years I have never needed a soft pad to sit upon. She shrugs and tucks a blanket around me.

Every day we wonder how Meg and the others are faring. Yet surprisingly I find myself content with my days spent here waiting for my leg to heal. I can't imagine having the strength to labour all day long on the Isle and think it unlikely I will ever join what Meg called her Middle Isle family, but we speak of visiting and seeing it for ourselves.

My daughter will remain over there, across the water, and I will stay here. While we are apart, I pray daily for her health and happiness, and then I thank the Lord for sending Joan to me.

# Jeb

Today I met my sister, Isabel. Her father carried her in his arms through the shallows to the shore, then placed her on the beach. As they approached, the first thing I noticed was that Isabel's hair is thick and golden, just how I remembered my mother's to be when she was a young woman.

"Here she is, your sister!" Alfred of Haven announced, and it sounded as if he would have liked her coming to be heralded by a trumpeter.

"Isabel – here he is! Your brother, Jeb!" my mother cried out in tandem as she clambered out of the boat, dropping into the sea which licked around her ankles.

My sister looked so small… so fragile, and I crouched to say, "Hello Isabel. Thank you for coming to see me." I didn't expect her to answer, but she gazed at me with her clear blue eyes and didn't shy away. "Thank you," I repeated, this time to my mother and Alfred. "I'm pleased you came back."

"Nothing could keep me away from my son," Mother responded immediately, rubbing her calves and feet with a piece of rough cloth.

"That's what I hoped," I replied, as they all continued drying themselves and replacing their stockings and shoes. "This is a strange thing for you all, coming to the Isle to find us living in this humble way. I've been lucky though; these people from Lydd are good folk and have accepted me as one of their own."

"They are lucky to have you," Alfred said.

"It was a lonely life before they came." The day before, we had spoken about my grandfather and how I had ended up living on Middle Isle. I planned this time with my family to be one of celebration and a chance to learn about their lives, so I continued, "But today is a great day in the history of this island – we have visitors from Hythe!"

"We must tell you about Hythe," Mother replied. "And the people of Hythe will hear about Middle Isle."

"I would like that."

We left the beach, walking slowly to match Isabel's pace towards the plots of worked land. I noticed that, in the short time I had been gone, Meg had left and was most likely at the creek washing her hands. Mine had been dunked in the water's edge on the beach and wiped on my tunic.

"Where is everyone?" Alfred asked.

"John has gone to Lydd," I told them. "Meg was here working with me, but it's our mealtime soon, so she'll be on her way back to their camp. There has been much change this morning – one of the tents has been taken down and the women will sleep in the longhouse tonight! We've been working on the house until late morning, until I thought it best to come here and watch for you all."

"I look forward to seeing it." Alfred turned to my mother, "Judith, isn't it interesting to be able to see a new settlement created?"

"It is," she responded. "Do you feel that you belong here, Jeb? Because we want you to know that we would like... that I hoped you would want to come to Hythe."

"There would be work and a home for you," Alfred added.

I don't remember a time when anyone had welcomed me in their life unless I think back to those early years when mother still lived in the old port of Romney. Now, in a short space of time, I had been accepted by the new settlers on Middle Isle and by my mother's husband. This offer to go with them to Hythe... It came too soon... I was not ready to leave the place which had become my home and the people I had met.

I was not ready to leave Meg.

They were looking at me. All three of them, although I couldn't be sure if Isabel understood. I had to reply and do so without causing any distress to my mother.

"Thank you," I began. "I hope you understand that I need to think about this. I'd expected to stay here and help farm this land and I'm not sure what these good people plan to do after the harvest – if some will stay or if they'll all return to Lydd. By then I hope to have decided about what to do next."

"You're needed here," Mother said. "We can see that."

"Judith, what would you think of your son if he deserted the people who have treated him with such kindness?" Alfred put his arm around my mother's shoulder and pulled her to him in a brief show of support and affection.

"I would think no less of him!"

"I know you wouldn't." I began to relax, grateful for his understanding. "Let me think about this while you are here. Let me think about coming to see you in Hythe."

"Nothing would make me happier than to leave here knowing I will see you again," My mother answered, and I knew she deserved that happiness.

By now we were passing the area with gnarled thorn trees, their earlier display of white and pink blossom now fading and fresh leaves emerging.

Skirting them, we neared the copse. Voices could be heard as everyone gathered for the midday meal.

"We brought gifts for Eve." Mother indicated the basket she carried. "Spices and herbs, some cheese and a smoked ham. It can't be easy to feed you all and now to have three strangers… It's too much."

"We have food coming from Lydd and fish… plenty of fish," I told her. "But a ham! Now that is something special. You're right, it's not easy, but everyone wants to see this venture work and they will work hard to make the harvest a success."

"I don't understand what led the fisherman to seek out your grandfather." Alfred's words took me back to yesterday and Daniel who had sought to make trouble for me.

"He was the only one who didn't want me to be a part of this." I gestured to the plots of land behind us. "He's gone now. Back to Lydd."

Alfred was left to ponder on this as, at that moment, Edwin spotted us and called a greeting, alerting the others who then gathered around my family, extending their welcome and encouraging them to sit for the meal.

Mother and Alfred understood their time here on Middle Isle was to be limited by the tide. After the meal we all lingered longer than usual, but the island settlers had to return to their various tasks – Meg and Luke to the land, Father Matthew to his holy place, Eve and Sarah to their chores within the camp, and Edwin to the longhouse.

The tide had turned, and my family needed to return to the new port of Romney. From there, they would begin their journey back to Hythe. They had the use of horses, Alfred told me, and could travel at a fair pace, with Isabel perched in front of her father. By nightfall they would be back in their own home.

Once more we found ourselves on the beach and now Isabel was in my arms. She still didn't say much but seemed happy to have met me, her big brother. I found myself charmed by her blue eyes, which seemed to watch me all the time and her golden curls bobbing about her shoulders.

"Let's find the very best shell on the beach," I suggested. "Then you can take it back with you and when you look at it you can remember me."

She nodded, and we set about exploring the ribbon of shells stretching out along the high tide mark. We discarded tiny pink slivers for, although they were the prettiest, they were also the most fragile. We rejected large specimens with rows of spikes for being too ugly, and cockle shells for being too ordinary. Then Isabel spotted a spiral of white with a glossy inside and flawlessly complete.

"This one," she declared.

"It's perfect. Let's show it to Mother."

"Look!" Isabel held the shell in a pincer grip and raised her arm upwards.

"It's lovely," my mother said, then turning to me. "Jeb, have you decided?"

"I'll stay here until the autumn," I told her. "There's someone here who is special to me and by then I will know if..."

"I'm sure she will!" Mother interrupted, taking me by surprise.

I smiled and shrugged. "After the first crops have been harvested, I'll come to Hythe and stay for a few days, if that suits you, and by then I'll know where my path lies." I looked at Alfred, and said, "I'm grateful for the offer of work and a home too. But I have a job to do here first."

"I understand, and like you all the better for it," he responded. "These people have been good to you, and we are glad to have spent time with them. I only regret not meeting with John again, but he has other business to attend to."

"And when you come to us, your wife will be as welcome as you are!" My mother stepped forward to give me a final hug. They had already removed their shoes and stockings as we stood at the water's edge.

I felt a blush rising through my neck and face as I wrapped my arms around Mother and mumbled a reply. Then I gave Alfred a brief embrace, placed a kiss on the top of Isabel's head and watched as they waded through the shallows to the waiting boat.

My family waved and called out until I could no longer see or hear them, but by then another boat was nearing the Isle. Two figures sat aboard, one being John and the other, presumably, the owner of the boat. The Middle Isle family, as I heard Meg call it, was about to have a new member.

# Meg

I watched as Jeb waved farewell to his family, then turned from the coast and, with long strides, made quick work of covering the ground between beach and plots. No sooner had he joined Luke and me than another boat had beached in the shallows.

"It's my father's!" Luke exclaimed. "And two men on board. Do you think it's...? It must be!" He stood on the edge of the newly marked-out plot with his back to our worked land and studied the men as they climbed out of the fishing boat and into the shallows. "It is!" And with that, Luke was bounding across the tussocks, the dips and the hillocks in the direction of the beach.

Looking at Jeb, I grinned. "This will be a rare day when we clear very little of our land. But your family have visited, and now Luke's father is here to join us." I shrugged. "It's still a good day!"

"And tomorrow we will work all the harder."

I leaned down to pick up a mass of fresh grass and tangled roots. The earth, solid and dry, felt heavy in my hands and fragments dropped to the ground as I walked to the edge of the plot. "Of course we will. Besides there has been such progress on the longhouse." I dropped the clod and turned, taking the few paces back towards Jeb. Reaching for the next load, I spotted movement nearby. "We have help! Friar Matthew is on his way."

"He is!" Jeb plunged the spade into the ground again, pushing it back and forth, loosening the compacted soil.

The monk set to work immediately, and we toiled with few words passing between us, continuing to keep an eye on the men on the beach. As soon as the boat had been pulled clear of the high tide mark, the three of them made their way towards us. Their voices carried on the light breeze, and I could sense Luke's eagerness. There was so much to share with his father who must be as keen to see the Isle as Luke was to show it. They paused for a moment as John, pointing in various directions, explained the lie of the land. The brief introduction over, they hastened towards us.

"Good day!" Samuel by Rother stood at the edge of our fourth plot. "Greetings, Friar Matthew." He lowered his gaze as a mark of respect, then raised his voice, "Hello Meg! I hear this land is just what you hoped for." Then he looked towards Jeb and continued, "And I hear great things about you! My son has just been telling me what a hard worker you are. It's good to meet you."

We all responded with enthusiasm, knowing already that Samuel by Rother would soon prove himself to be a valued member of our Middle Isle family.

"What do you have here?" Samuel asked. "Three plots of fertile soil and all planted with seeds, I know. But what will be filling our cooking pot by the time the summer is with us?"

John led him to the pathway between the first and second plots and pointed to the third. "There's barley in that one, newly planted in the last few days, and it will be the same in the fourth area, which we hope to have cleared and prepared within a week. These here have seeds in them. Tell him Meg..."

"The turnip and parsnip were sown first over there," I pointed in the direction of an evenly raked patch. "Then onion bulbs over there.   A week later we put the carrot seeds next to the onion, and then peas right here."

"And now we wait for them to sprout." Luke stood at the edge of the first plot and stared intently at the soil. "Meg, is this...?" He crouched and pointed.

I knelt next to him, scanning the earth where he indicated. There it was! The first tender pea shoot emerging. Suddenly the more I looked, the more I could see. So tiny, so fragile, but new growth, nonetheless. "Pea shoots!" I cried out. "John! Jeb! Here they are – our first crop!"

Raising myself, I turned to Luke. "Come on..." Racing along the dividing pathway, I rounded the end of the first plot and stopped at the outer edge before once more dropping to my knees and searching the earth for the signs of fresh growth. I was immediately rewarded with the sight of tiny heart-shaped leaves, open to catch the warmth of the sun. "The turnips have sprouted!"

On this day that Samuel by Rother joined our Middle Isle family, peace has been restored. Jebediah looks more comfortable than I have ever seen him before. He is a man with two families now and he knows he is accepted by both. We have spotted the first signs of growth and every person in our group has made the pilgrimage, first to admire the heart-shaped turnip leaves and rounded pea shoots, then to the friar's altar to share his offerings of thanks.

# *Meg*
## Midsummer

Today, with the help of local fishermen, the people of Lydd came to our island – boatload after boatload of them.

As soon as the tide reached its midway point on the beach, Samuel and Luke pushed their vessel out to meet it and set off across the Rother. Then they were back, joined by other boats, each one full of our kinfolk. As we greeted our visitors, we helped them through the shallows and thanked them over and over for the number of wicker baskets and wooden boxes laden with a variety of food stuffs. The fishermen turned their boats about, ready to repeat the journey, bringing more of our friends and family. It has been an exhausting day for them.

Before long, it felt as if the Isle had been invaded. Not one lonely creek, patch of ground, shaded area of copse or strip of beach remained untouched by our family and friends. John and I knew we must remain by the crops – each one now thriving and lush – to explain over and over our methods and the progress made here.

"Aye, we've been here three cycles of the moon," I could hear John saying as he stood amongst the three plots of barley. "It's beginning to ripen and when the cabbage and peas are fully harvested, we'll plant the winter crop over there. Barley doesn't mind the salt air, you see. It's growing well."

Of all the places in Middle Isle, one of my favourite spots to stand is on one of our narrow pathways between the ripening barley. I love the way it sways in the breeze, catching the long, wispy fronds which encase the seedhead. The herringbone patterned heads remain resolutely green but over the coming weeks they will dry and turn golden brown.

We have eight half-acre plots now and space for more. Two of them are empty, awaiting the winter oats. Here on Middle Isle we gain satisfaction from everything we have done, and try to not feel frustration over the areas, as yet, unseeded.

I stood amongst the rambling peas. How different this crop is from the upright, orderly barley. The rounded leaves face this way and that, and spiralling tendrils doggedly seek opportunities to cling to nearby stalks. White flowers blossom amongst new growth, while lower down the plant stems, seedheads have formed and pods of sweet peas mature.

"We've been picking these for the last month," I tell the fascinated visitors. "Have you tried them?" After months of receiving food from Lydd, we are finally able to return the favour.

"Over there, you can see the carrots and turnips, and there the cabbages..." These vegetables are not as attractive, but we keep the areas free from weeds as best we can, and I gain pleasure from seeing the orderly rows. Carrots, long, slender and white, were harvested only yesterday, while bulbous, purple-topped turnips gained the honour of being the first crop to mature here. Cabbages, never a favourite with their small tough leaves, are nonetheless essential and provide sustenance during the lean times.

"What's over there? Onions?"

"Aye, onions."

And so it continued... From my place amongst the peas, I watched the cycle of boats arriving, the passengers paddling through the shallows, and the fishermen leaving once more for Lydd. They worked hard that day, those men rowing the six boats. I could see eager faces turned as the folk from Lydd gazed towards Middle Isle, greedy for details of the Isle, eager to see where we had been living for these past months.

At last, I spotted my father, his gait awkward but back straight and head held high as he stepped onto the sand and pebbles for the first time. I saw him pointing and speaking to Joan whose arm was tucked into his. Then I left my post with the peas and ran across the uneven ground, confident that I knew each dip and tussock well enough that I could be at the top of the beach as Father and Joan reached it.

"Welcome!" I called as we met on the edge of the grassland. "Welcome to Middle Isle." Father and I hugged in an awkward manner, this not being our usual way of greeting each other.

"At last!" Father replied.

"We are eager to see it all," Joan told me.

"I'm eager to show it to you." I hadn't seen Joan on the one occasion I had returned to Lydd, but I knew she had helped my father through some of his darkest times. I stepped forward and took her hands in mine. "Thank you. Thank you for taking care of him."

Over time, we have trodden tracks across the grassland and now, after exchanging words about their boat journey and first impressions, Father, Joan and I followed the path back to the plots.

"At last, we can see it for ourselves," Father exclaimed. "Look at it all. Just look at how well the crops grow – how lush their leaves, how strong their stems." He appeared to brace himself for a movement which no longer came naturally to him, bent down a little, and then grumbled, "Dammit, nothing comes as easily as it used to. Joan, could you... I'd like to feel the earth in my hand."

"Every day it is a little easier," she reassured him, crouching to take a pinch of earth from amongst the barley.

With the earth in his palm, Father crumbled it between his fingers, letting it fall to the ground. "It is good."

"A little dry at the moment," I said. "We've had no rain these past few days, but so far we have been lucky, very lucky, with the weather."

Leaving the barley, we tramped every path between the crops, until Father was satisfied that he had inspected each area, whether planted or being prepared for the first seeds. He paused to speak to John, still stationed with the fronds of barley, and met Jeb, who guided our visitors amongst the turnips, carrots and onions.

"He's a good worker," Father declared, having paused to speak to Jeb. "That's what you need here – strong men who will work without complaint."

"He's a good man too," Joan added. "His face is kind and his manner gentle."

A sensation of warmth flooded through me. My friendship with Jeb has strengthened over the past months and I want my father to approve. But not only my father – I sense that Joan is going to be another important person in my life, and I am glad to know that she sees the goodness in Jeb.

From the plots we headed first to the creek, and then to the copse, barely walking any distance at all before stopping to speak with someone visiting from Lydd. Everyone wanted to express their thoughts or ask about my experiences.

"Here it is – the longhouse!" Father announced as we neared the copse. His stride lengthened and back straightened, so eager was he to see how we lived. "And Edwin made all this!"

"With help," I added. "But it was his design, and he has worked tirelessly on our shelters, whereas the rest of us concentrated mostly on the land."

People were queuing to peer into the rooms where we slept. I pulled back, feeling no need to point out each compartment. Over time, we had come to an arrangement: The two married couples each have their own area, while Luke and his father, Samuel, share and I have my own small space. As planned, we keep the central area of the longhouse open to the front and back. This is where our fire burns, and we gather to eat. Friar Matthew has chosen his own place under the trees and now sleeps under the sloping sides of a humble wooden structure.

Our guests sat where they could, on blankets they had brought with them, on makeshift benches hewn from planks sawn by Edwin or on logs. On their knees, they balanced wooden plates which they filled with food selected from our table: cheese, smoked ham, pickled vegetables and mutton pies – all delicacies for us on Middle Isle – brought from Lydd for the occasion. These accompanied mussels collected from our own shore, and mackerel caught by Samuel the day before. French wine from Amory of Langport's own store filled our beakers, while any desire for sweet foods was satisfied with honeyed biscuits and apple pies.

"Is it too much for you?" Joan asked my father, as we prepared to trail behind Friar Matthew and our priest from Lydd to give our thanks at his altar.

"I would walk to Romney if that was where the monk led me," Father replied. "We must give our thanks for this land. Besides, I can rest again before the journey home."

"Aye, we have time for both," she agreed. For the visitors, this was no fleeting visit. They were to remain on Middle Isle until the tide rose once more.

With the summer sun beating down upon us, and barely a wisp of cloud visible in the sky, we left the shade of the copse to follow Friar Matthew to his holy place at the highest point of the Isle. The chatter ceased, and we crowded around to watch as the town's priest stood alongside the friar on the sandy rise. Standing between Father and Joan, I gazed across the mudflats to the river forging its way to the coast. Sluggish waters glittered and Romney shimmered in the heat haze. The monk's words rose and fell, melodic and soothing.

Afterwards, those who wanted to ramble about the place did so, as others settled back in the shade. Someone pulled a whistle from a bag, another produced a timbrel, and we sang songs telling the stories of the seasons, the land and our ancestors.

I glanced towards Jeb as he tapped his hand on his knee to the beat of the timbrel. At that moment, his gaze fell on me and he smiled.

# Martin

I don't think about the Normans now or how I believed that Amory wanted to banish me from Lydd. My leg still causes me some discomfort and I'll suffer for it during the cold, damp winters, but my heart is filled with joy.

Joan has agreed to be my wife! We are going to speak to the priest tomorrow. I asked her when we returned from Middle Isle. She tolerates my stubborn ways very well and I find that, when we are together, life doesn't seem so difficult. We laugh and we talk: I am learning about the places she has seen in her travels, and we speak of journeying to the west to visit the hilltop town of Rye, and to the east to see the church being built in the new port of Romney. I have presented her with the loom I made when she was out tending the goats and chickens and collecting the honey. Despite being hindered by my weak leg, I managed to buy, through the lad who works my land, a selection of coloured wools. The loom and wool made a fine gift for a woman who has been both caring and helpful during the time my daughter has been away.

Yesterday, on our visit to the island, Joan made sure I didn't give all my attention to the crops. "Martin, I think you should get to know Jebediah, Jeb…. Speak to him and learn about his life here." I can't pretend I knew why she suggested this when there was so much to look at and such little time, but I did.

I found him to be a fine young man. He and Meg have worked well together for several cycles of the moon, both on the field and turning his fleece to yarn. Their friendship has grown, and I can see how much he is liked within the Middle Isle family. Meg is of an age when she should marry and discover the joy of loving companionship.

Once my decision had been made, and with the tide rising, I hastened to speak to my daughter before we had to leave. "At last, I have set eyes on a husband good enough for you!"

"A husband?" She frowned. Meg is like me, thinking only of the soil and crops.

"Jebediah is a good man. Hardworking and kind."

She smiled. "Aye, he is."

The people from Lydd were preparing to leave now, making their way to the beach. There was little chance to say more. "You'll leave here after the harvest, Meg. Come home to Lydd with a husband.

Marry him here! As long as he has a gift to offer, then he can pledge his love and the vow is binding. Wait if you like, but you must grasp happiness while you can. And if you choose to make a new life in Hythe, then I hear it is a fine town and I'll be happy for you."

By now we were heading for the boats. Meg remained quiet for a moment, no doubt surprised by the words spilling from me. Then, having reached the shoreline, she gave me a hug and said, "Jeb is a good man, the best. Thank you for your blessing."

Two men took the oars, and others raised the sail. We were quite a crowd on board, but I managed to keep my eyes focussed on my only child as the distance grew between us.

It appeared to me, and Joan agreed, that Meg and Jeb were standing close together as they waved in our direction. It seems to me that my daughter is not too old to accept her father's advice.

# *The End*

# Thanks

Thank you to everyone who supports my writing through buying my novels and attending workshops, and to the local stockists. Many thanks to my friends and family who are so understanding about the huge amount of time I need to spend creating novels, workshops and talks.

# *Coming up...*

Midley – Five Gold Coins
Canterbury & Midley 14th century
(estimated publication late autumn 2024)

Midley - Abandoned (working title)
Locations undecided 16th century
(estimated publication spring 2025)

Midley – At War (working title)
Lydd & Midley 1940s
(estimated publication summer 2025)